Florentia and the Pazzi Boy

A novella

Florentia and the Pazzi Boy

a Renaissance fable

Second Edition

Ralph Feliciello

Second Edition

Cover Graphics: miyakoistudio@gmail.com

Author photo: www.konboogie.com

KNT Publishing / New York

To

Katherine
and
Nicholas

Author's Note

This fable was born of two historical facts.

The first is that in April of 1478 conspirators, hoping to end the Medici family's domination of the nominal republic of Florence, attempted to assassinate Lorenzo de' Medici and his brother Giuliano during Easter Mass in the cathedral. Lorenzo was not severely injured, though Giuliano died bleeding from nineteen stab wounds at the foot of the altar. In the aftermath, Medici vengeance claimed over one hundred lives.

Giuliano's killer, Bernardo Baroncelli, escaped for a time. Tracked down in Constantinople by Medici agents, he was brought back in chains and executed.

The leader of the conspiracy, Jacopo de' Pazzi, was hanged from a high window of Palazzo della Signoria, the seat of power where he had envisioned himself lifted to the throne of glory. His body was cut down, dragged through the streets, and tossed into the Arno River.

The second historical fact is that Jacopo de' Pazzi sired a child out of wedlock.

The facts end here.

Table of Contents

Prologue: Orphaned at Birth

Easter Sunday

The young kitchen maid had felt unwell on waking. Though the mistress of Palazzo Pazzi usually allowed her favorite servant to join the family at Sunday Mass, that morning Signora Pazzi advised the girl to keep to her bed. "My dear Desislava, you are young. There will be many more Sundays when you—"

"But this is Easter Sunday," pouted the girl, sitting up straight in bed to show she was not so ill after all.

"—when, as I was saying," continued La Signora, "you can show the young gallants of Florence how wonderful you look in the dress that hasn't fit me since I was your age."

"But I might die any minute," Desislava pointed out, quite rightly. "My forehead is burning up. My eyebrows are about to go up in flames, then my hair will catch fire, and—"

"What is this about a fever? You said stomach ache," chided La Signora, placing a caring hand on the girl's forehead. "Hmmm. You will live. At least until next Sunday." The disappointed girl fell back on the bed and stretched herself out, stiff as a corpse.

La Signora stopped by the kitchen on her way out to instruct the old cook to look in on Desislava. Then the women, children, and elders of the Pazzi clan poured out onto Via del Proconsolo, passing with pride beneath the family's sculpted coat of arms—two leaping dolphins—on the palazzo's façade.

They were without the family patriarch, Ser Jacopo de' Pazzi, who the day before had ridden to Pisa on business, or so he told his wife.

. . .

Desislava, feeling ill, forsaken, and alone, pressed her face to the pillow and squeezed out a tear. She fell asleep to pass the time. Hours later, she awoke knowing, even with eyes shut, that she was alone, while every other young girl in Florence was celebrating probably the most beautiful day of the year, maybe of her whole life. Restless, Desislava quit her narrow bed and made her way to the tall windows of the palazzo's noble front room hung with portraits of honored ancestors—not her ancestors. Desislava had no ancestors.

Joyful voices of Easter revelers reached her ears, as a grand religious procession filled the street below. Yet it was an unholy rite she witnessed, for a mob was dragging a man over the cobblestones by a rope around his neck. They set the man upright and shoved him against the palazzo door directly below. Desislava murmured, "I know that man. That is Ser Jacopo. Why are those people being so cruel to him? They must be punishing him for what he did to me last summer." And the memory of what the man had done to her that August morning when he found the girl alone returned the fever to her head. She padded back to the servants' quarters, but on nearing her bed, a sharp ache stiffened her back. Something moved very deep inside her. A strange new pain pressed her to the wall. The floor rose up. She felt the wetness of the tiles on the back of her legs. She heard a baby's cry. She was crying. She cried out for La Signora.

. . .

Signora Pazzi was in the cathedral, weeping. Such a privilege for La Signora, among thirty thousand worshippers, to have been ushered to a place so near the altar. But she would give anything not to have been kneeling so close to the stabbing of Giuliano de' Medici that, moments later, she discovered two drops of the victim's blood on the sleeve of her dress.

The Captain of the Guard had ordered the massive cathedral cleared, the doors sealed, and Signora Pazzi and her kin locked in a side chapel where spearmen prodded them against a fresco of the Last Judgment, the children less frightened by the tortures of the damned than by the look of terror in their elders' eyes.

Lorenzo de' Medici himself had commanded that no Pazzi be allowed to leave the cathedral until the Captain of the Guard was certain he had separated the guilty from the merely disgraced. All Florence feared being interrogated by the Captain at the Bargello prison where he was known for using a red-hot iron, wrought into the outline of the Lily of Florence, which never failed to extract the truth from lying tongues. He was also known for a skin condition that caused him to sweat even in the cold, and on that Easter Sunday the cathedral was as hot as a forge.

After his repeated demands for a full confession from La Signora yielded only tearful pleas of innocence, the Captain brought his face—as moist with sweat as hers was with tears—within an inch of the lady's, and said, "With all respect, Signora, you are a liar."

"No, Captain, I am not."

"And your husband Jacopo is not just an old satyr, as everyone knows, but a traitor to the Republic."

"As I told you a hundred times, my husband is in Pisa on business to do with the Pazzi bank."

"I know better, you know better, and by now, all Florence knows better. You sit there knowing full well that this morning your husband, the old sinner, was not in Pisa making a deposit with his mistress, but—"

"My husband, Sir, is a sinner, I confess, and you are the devil."

The Captain, pleased by the compliment, smiled, ordered La Signora to stand, and kicked the chair out from under her. Stumbling, she steadied herself against a marble column and heard, "You will stand at that pillar till next Easter or until—"

At that moment a messenger entered the chapel and whispered in the Captain's ear. What the Captain heard first hardened then softened his features. Even before he had put his first question to La Signora, the Captain was aware that Ser Jacopo, riding through the cobbled streets declaring himself the liberator of Florence, was pulled from his horse and delivered to the magistrates who delighted the pro-Medici mob by hanging their failed liberator from a high window of Palazzo della Signoria.

The messenger now informed the Captain that Ser Jacopo's body had been cut down and turned over to the mob that dragged it over the cobblestones to his palazzo door then, with a cheer, tossed his lifeless body into the flood-muddied Arno River and watched it disappear. The Captain was not pleased to learn that Jacopo, before his execution, as the noose rested around his neck, spent his last breath swearing that his wife knew nothing of the conspiracy.

The Captain dismissed the messenger and told Signora Pazzi, "You are free to go. But, be warned, you have not seen the last of me."

La Signora replied, "Your messenger no doubt assured you that my husband was in no way involved with the bloody sacrilege that took place here."

"Your husband, as you say, Signora, is in Pisa on business. When he returns, we will have a few questions to ask him. For the present, my soldiers will see that you and the family arrive safely at your palazzo door. Good day, Signora. I wish you all the joy of the Easter season. And may your reunion with Ser Jacopo be one you will long remember."

A Father's Embrace

The bronze doors of the cathedral swung open to the sun and a searing hatred of anyone unfortunate enough on that day to carry the Pazzi name. Guardsmen did nothing to protect Signora Pazzi and her kin from the pokes and taunts chasing them down Via del Proconsolo. La Signora's prayer book, lifted to her face, could not shield her from the spittle of those who that morning had bowed to her as she passed.

Soldiers on horseback hurried to protect a priest jostled in the crowd. "That priest," angry voices yelled, "should be made to march with the Pazzi! We've seen him with them!" Twice the clergyman denied knowing the Pazzi. But his accusers shouted him down with, "He serves them in the Pazzi Chapel!" Before the priest could add a third denial, Signora Pazzi, waving her prayer book, called out to him by name. "Father Enzo! Father Enzo! Pray for me!"

The black cassock, pushed from the crowd, was soon marching alongside La Signora.

. . .

Signora Pazzi, with the children and elders of the clan, arrived at the palazzo to find the servants had abandoned their posts on hearing fists banging against the main entrance and chants of, "Death to the Pazzi and all who support them!" The terrified old cook left Desislava to her fate, even knowing the girl's condition and who had fathered that condition, an unkept secret she heralded through the streets as she fled.

The family, now embraced by familiar walls, with ancestors smiling down from gilded frames, moistened each other's cheeks with tears, a moment of peace shattered by the smashing of a window. Picking through broken glass, they found not a rock but a stone fragment from the Pazzi coat of arms pulled down from the facade. The fragment, one of the two leaping dolphins, passed from hand to hand, until all movement stopped at the sound of a baby's cry. The cry was coming from the servants' quarters.

Signora Pazzi was the first to discover that Death, satisfied with taking Desislava after giving birth, had spared her newborn. Death must have been tempted to take the life of the baby also, for the birth cord was wound tight around its neck, choking its cries but unable to silence them. La Signora tended to the baby, while stronger arms placed the unfortunate Desislava on her narrow bed beneath a simple, wooden cross. Father Enzo administered the Last Rites.

The baby, cleaned, swaddled, and gurgling the tiniest of bubbles, was carried to the bed to share the pillow with its mother. A white-haired elder asked, "What is to become of the child?" All heads bowed, pitying the poor creature. But the old man's next words—"The boy is not one of us"—raised eyebrows, for everyone knew of Ser Jacopo's goatish ways.

Signora Pazzi, long aware that her husband battled like Saint Anthony against what she preferred to call concupiscence, had seen to it that Ser Jacopo dropped to his knees regularly behind the red velvet curtain of the confessional in the Pazzi Chapel. And so, she turned to Father Enzo, the family's confessor, and parted her lips to speak, intending to ask if he had heard, over the last nine months, anything that might settle the question of the baby's paternity. She hesitated, not wishing to tempt the priest into betraying the seal of secrecy. During that pause, a young woman placed the baby in the priest's arms, saying, "I will speak for my sister. Please, Father Enzo, bring this child to the Foundling Home."

"No, no," cried La Signora. "No, dear Monica, we will not abandon Desislava's baby. I would rather that we—"

She was silenced by a great pounding at the palazzo door. The priest, with the baby in his rather stiff embrace, remained in the servants' quarters, while the others clambered downstairs, arriving as spear-wielding guardsmen burst through the double doors. In strode the Captain of the Guard waving a document, demanding silence, and declaring, "I am here to deliver Lorenzo's judgment concerning the family. I must be brief, for your sake."

He began reading from the document: "Under pain of death...," but had to stop to call again for silence. Then he continued, "...every citizen of Pazzi blood must be beyond the walls of Florence before the sun slips behind the western hills. You will be allowed to bring into exile only what you are able to carry. The soldier-for-hire condottiere known as The Black Death will escort you through the streets and out the Porta alla Croce where carriages with fresh horses will carry you beyond Florentine territory. Since no city in Italy will risk Medici wrath by offering sanctuary, you must journey over the Alps to France."

The Captain wiped the sweat from his brow with the document, let it fall to the floor, said, "I bid you all *au revoir et bon voyage*," and marched out. Guardsmen closed ranks behind him, pounding the base of their spears against porcelain flooring tiles showing the Pazzi coat of arms, splitting apart each pair of leaping dolphins. Slamming double doors sealed the family's fate.

A moment later, the doors reopened. Two stable boys entered and stood before Signora Pazzi, caps in hand, to offer information they were very sorry to report. First, they were proud to say that they had not run away like the other servants but, instead, had roamed the streets, yelling, "Death to all Pazzi traitors!" the better to intercept news the family might need to hear. The older of the two boys picked up the trampled document from the floor, not knowing what it was, and handed it to La Signora. She thanked the boy, adding, "And what did you learn in the streets? Please be brief."

The boys recited, in unison, these well-practiced words: "We learned that news reached Lorenzo in Palazzo Medici that this very morning a kitchen maid gave birth to Ser Jacopo's natural child."

The boys fell silent.

La Signora asked, "Is there more?"

"There is, Signora."

"Please, go on."

Together the boys said, "These are Lorenzo's words which we heard from someone who heard them from someone who was in the room with him when he said them." The younger boy, not wishing to wound La Signora with words still to be said, lowered his head and spoke no more. His companion stepped forward. "What I will say now is spoken by Lorenzo, not me, dear Lady."

"I understand," she said.

Then he recited: "The soul of my brother Giuliano will not rest until I can stand on a bridge of the Arno and watch Jacopo's little bastard sinking to a deep sleep in his dear father's arms."

Ralph Feliciello

Part One: A Kiss by the Window

Chapter 1

Iride Means Rainbow

R enato and Placido, fast friends, sat side by side on the ruins of the sea-washed Roman baths on Pianosa Island, tossing pebbles at their enemy the horizon, every pebble plopping short of its target. Dangling their feet at the water's edge, they glanced down at the wavelets whitewashing their toes, the way Renato had whitewashed the cemetery shed early that morning, at his father's command.

"The Roman baths on this island consisted of a tepidarium, a caldarium, and a frigidarium," explained Placido, nicknamed The Professor, because, having blown the dust off every book in the library of the rectory where he lived, he always spoke as if he were delivering a lecture on Roman history. As Father Enzo said of Placido, "I can always find him in the study, using his nose as a bookmark."

Renato's skills, in contrast, were not of the professorial but the broad-shouldered kind learned from the backbreaking work of making Pianosa's graveyard a fit place for a body to rest. Since reaching half his current age of eighteen, Renato alone had worked the stony cemetery ground. The boy's father had not picked up a shovel for many years. The man walked bent forward at the waist, his back nearly parallel with the ground. He groped along, jabbing and cursing at the earth with his cane, believing it was the earth that broke his back in revenge for all the times he broke the earth's back, digging graves. The boys referred to him, behind his back, as the Gibbet, another word for the gallows still standing at the hilltop prison shuttered long ago due to an outbreak of the plague.

The two friends enjoyed giving others a second name. Renato's mother's elfin stature earned her the nickname Childwoman. Father Enzo was known as the Raven, because of the cassock that blackened him from the neck down.

The name given in the baptismal records for Placido's sister was Florentia, the Latin term for the ancient Roman settlement of Florence, because her mother had prayed that this daughter of a rectory housekeeper and a prison guard would one day become the fine signora of a Florentine palazzo. Renato's name for Florentia was Iride, which means rainbow, because of her red hair and eyes of different colors, one blue, one green. Those eyes had once struck Renato as strange, unnatural. But, not so very long ago, he reasoned that if the sky could have two different colored eyes, so could a girl. And lately, he had found himself, leaning against the tool shed or sitting high in a tree, wondering what it would be like to look into those eyes, at close range. But Iride moved in the rare atmosphere of the rectory, with books on shelves and paintings on walls. She would never allow the touch of a hand soiled by the dust of dead men's bones.

"You didn't hear a word I said, did you, Renato?" asked Placido. "No, you didn't, because you're dreaming again. I was saying that Augustus Caesar ordered Rome's finest artisans to build on this island a magnificent temple to Venus, Goddess of Love, though we've never found one stone of it. Venus was born fully formed from the foam of the sea and floated to shore on a half shell, wearing nothing but a bracelet."

"What color was her hair?"

"Her hair? I don't know. Probably black. In the woodcuts, her hair is always black."

Renato imagined the color of Venus's hair to be the brilliant shade of red the inside of his eyelids became when he closed them and lifted his face to the sun. He had earned the name, The Dreamer, because of his way of never settling for reality when a more believable world was just a thought away. Though Renato's baptismal name meant reborn, Florentia and Placido christened him John the Baptist, because of his long hair and love of roaming over the far side of the island they called the wilderness. But the nickname Renato felt suited him best was Amerigo, because he never stopped believing that one day he would sail to the New World, where native peoples live simply, with respect for the Earth. He now reminded Placido, for the fourteen hundred and ninety-fourth time this year, "I will get to the New World some day, if I have to swim there."

"You're not going anywhere, Pulcinella," said the grave voice of the Gibbet, and Renato felt his father's knobby cane pressing down on his shoulder. The pain was slight compared to the sting of his father's favorite name for him, Pulcinella, a straw-headed dunce of the Commedia dell'Arte, a wandering troupe of zany characters.

The bent-over man twisted his neck to fix an eye on his son. "I told you this morning to fetch more firewood. Don't make me come looking for you again," he warned, then, pointing with his cane to the cemetery high on the hill, he jabbed his way up the slope to the bluff, expecting his son to follow. And Renato followed because he had promised his ailing mother that he would be an obedient son, until the day he could swim away, like the stranded sea turtle he had set down where the sand ended and the water of freedom began.

At the cemetery shed, the Gibbet ordered Renato to put away the whitewash and brush that the boy had used early that morning. "Do that, then come back here to me," he said. Renato carried the whitewash and brush into the shed, then walked back and stood before his father. The Gibbet told him to gather some dirt in his hand. Renato bent down and then straightened up, showing his father the dirt in his hand.

"More dirt," ordered the Gibbet. Renato added more dirt. "My son," said the Gibbet, "I don't want to hear any more talk from you about leaving this island for the New World. We are all going to die on this island, you, me, and your mother. That is our fate. You were born on this island, just like me, and here you will breathe your last and here be buried, to look up to heaven through the stone-choked dirt of this graveyard." The Gibbet ordered Renato to open his mouth. Renato did not, at first—then he obeyed. "Put the dirt in your mouth," said the Gibbet. Renato obeyed. "Now, swallow." When the boy remained close-mouthed, the Gibbet dropped his cane, grabbed the boy, and began working his jaw to make him swallow. The boy eased his father's hands away and then, with a look, gave him to understand he would do as he was told. Renato swallowed the dirt, scooped up even more than before, placed it in his mouth, and swallowed. The Gibbet said, "Good. Now, this island is a part of you. Go, gather the firewood your mother needs to cook your next meal."

That evening in the cemetery shack Renato's mother, the Childwoman, set before him a wooden bowl that remained untouched. The Childwoman, in a pained voice that her worsening illness reduced to a strained whisper, asked the boy why he was not eating his soup. He answered that he was not hungry and made his way down the hill to stand at the edge of the bluff.

The Dreamer fixed his eyes on the sun until it disappeared, and sea and sky darkened to a woodcut. He waited for Venus to come floating toward him on a half shell. But only the Moon appeared. Turning to leave, he noticed a silhouette among the distant shadows. A darker silhouette overlapped the first, then moved away. The first silhouette grew larger as it came toward the bluff. Renato dropped so close to the ground he tasted dirt on his tongue. The silhouette was almost upon him when he witnessed the slender fingers of the Moon lifting the veil of darkness from the face of the girl he had renamed Iride.

All at once the black canopy of night filled with stars lighting the way for Iride moving down the slope and into the sea, an undulating mirror of the overhanging stars now floating on the water. The Moon descended toward Iride, as if their meeting had been planned. As Iride waded forward, the bobbing stars rose all around her, until she presented herself beneath the Moon wearing a mantle of watery, shape-changing stars. A mysterious communication passed between Iride and the Moon. Then Iride waded back toward shore, the starry mantle slipping from her shoulders.

The Moon ascended. A sudden wind blew out the stars, and Iride hurried up the slope where Renato saw that she was trembling and heard her tears as she walked past, to darken again to a silhouette, that became a distant shadow, soon lost in the blackness all around.

Chapter 2

In The Charnel House

R enato found the Childwoman sitting on the front step of the cemetery shack, his wooden bowl of soup beside her.

"You're trembling," he said. "You'll catch a chill."

"It's cold," she said.

"You shouldn't be sitting out here."

"Your soup. It got cold. Come, sit with me," she said, patting the step beside her. "I forgot the spoon."

"You should be inside, in bed."

"Sit down, Renato. I have something to tell you." He sat beside his mother, and she said, "Your father says the evening meal is the only pleasure he has left. The man has not had an easy life."

"No."

"He has a bad heart."

"Yes."

"He doesn't want you eating at the table with us anymore."

"I can eat out here on the step."

"He doesn't want you sleeping in the shack anymore. He said for you to clean out the charnel house and sleep there."

"And what did you say to him, Mother?"

"I said it will be better for both of you. The man has a bad heart. He can't take any more pain. You can. You're young. You have your whole life ahead of you. What does your father have ahead of him? You have to feel sorry for the man. He spent his whole life digging graves. Do you know what it does to a person year after year to take up the lifeless body when loved ones turn away, and it is up to you to cover it with dirt like something the dog left behind? Whatever you think of him, that man is your father."

Renato accepted his banishment to the charnel house. That house of bones held no terrors for him. Bones were his first playthings. As an infant, on the countless mornings his bedridden mother spent pressing a crucifix to her breast, baby Renato would crawl after his father from grave to grave in the cemetery. Later, as a young boy, bones were to Renato what books were to Placido. They taught him what he needed to know about life.

Renato spent the first hour in his new home sitting on broken flooring stones looking at three heaps of what remains of human beings after Time has eaten its fill—one heap of large bones, one of small, and one pyramid of skulls looking shocked at what had become of them, each skull angled a little differently while asking the wall or the ceiling or the floor, "How could it all have come to this?"

Renato stuffed many burlap sacks with thigh bones that once kept men upright but were now useful only as cudgels to split open other men's heads—and all the other bones tossed up over the years by floods or quakes or the insistence of the next tenant. With a tilt of the wheelbarrow, sack after sack of dusty bones fell to the bottom of the sinkhole at the back of the cemetery.

But Renato did not empty the charnel house of every bone. He kept back a special selection that he laid out on the floor to form a complete skeleton, for he knew the human framework so well, it was as if he had been there watching on Day Three as the Creator laid out Adam's bones, one by one, in the mud of Eden.

Before Renato's eyes the bones he laid out on the floor of the charnel house took on a human form, the form of a particular human, and he stepped very carefully so as not to disturb Iride, asking her to please wait for him while he left her alone a moment. In the tool shed, with hammer and nail, he punched many holes in a flat piece of tin that he fashioned into a lantern, complete with a door, a handle, and a place inside for a small candle. Rushing back to the one who waited for him, he set the lantern down beside her, lit the candle, and, through the holes in every surface, beams of starlight shot out in all directions. He turned the lantern, and the stars turned—on the ceiling, on the walls, on the floor, and across Iride's hair and eyes. Renato lay down beside her. He was the first to speak. "You didn't see me, but I was on the bluff when you waded out to speak with the moon. Afterward, you rushed right past me, and I could tell you were crying. I cry, too. It's this island. Someday, you and I will leave together, and we won't stop until we get to the New World. Yes, you're right. That takes money, a lot of money. But when I was clearing out the bones, I found something very valuable. Under some broken floor tiles, I found a hole I widened to show a stairway going down. On the top step was something small and round—a gold coin. With a little spit, I rubbed it clean enough to see the face of a Roman emperor who will pay our way to the New World. Would you like to see it?"

Iride did not answer. She had fallen asleep. Renato opened the small door of the lantern and blew out the stars. Tired deep in his bones, he lay back, pillowing his head on a broken floor tile, and soon became one with the darkness all around.

The Black Death

"Wake up, Renato! Wake up! Wake up!" The boy half opened one eye. A man's face was bending over him, ordering him to get up and start working. It was Enzo, the Raven, his jittery black shoes scattering the bones across the floor. "You have to carry away the body! I've got to perform the Last Rites! The Black Death, he's here! Medici agents found Baroncelli hiding in Constantinople, Bernardo Baroncelli who stabbed Giuliano. There's going to be a hanging. Bring the wagon. Now! The Black Death won't be kept waiting!"

Renato, eyelids heavy with sleep, trudged to the shed, rolled out the wagon, and, walking between the shafts, started up the steep road leading to the abandoned prison. Before long he stopped to let Enzo catch his breath.

"Wait! I want to come, too!" shouted Placido running up the rutted road. Enzo yelled, "Go back. Go back home. Do as I tell you." And the obedient boy turned a sour face toward the rectory.

Renato, with Enzo trailing behind, continued up the hill, the sun baking their backs. They rested before the fortress-like prison rising on the hilltop closest to the sun. Deep shadows of the barrel-vaulted entranceway painted Enzo's cassock a darker shade of black. From the prison courtyard came clipped commands and the clatter of horses' hooves on cobblestones. Enzo, grabbing Renato's arm, said, "Let me do the talking. Remember, I'll do the talking." Then, catching sight of disobedient Placido ducking behind the wagon, Enzo gave the boy's ear a twist that sent him squealing back down the hill. Suddenly, a black-bearded soldier filled the archway. "You two, follow me!" shot from his mouth like the salvos of a cannon, and Renato and Enzo passed from the darkness of the entranceway into the squinting sun. The cannon-voiced soldier joined his fellows in the ranks, and all turned to the center of the courtyard, where stood a magnificent black stallion ridden by a knight whose open visor revealed the face not of a killer but of a killer of killers. Here was the Medici-hired condottiere known throughout Italy as The Black Death because everyone believed he had filled more coffins than the plague.

The knight needed only a touch of the reins to command the great stallion to rise up and claw the air. Renato was seeing an equestrian statue come to life. Suddenly, the mighty bronze horse jumped from the marble pedestal, its powerful head swinging so close to Renato's face that frightened eyes and bulging eyes regarded one another, while the knight's longsword sliced through the air. "He is the Pazzi Boy! Seize him!" Soldiers dragged Renato to the gallows where a dangling noose hung ready.

"You're making a mistake, Sir," a voice called out from the entranceway. "That boy was born on this island. I've known him all my life." Florentia stepped into the courtyard, shielding her eyes from the sun.

"Don't you worry, young lady," said the condottiere, sheathing his sword. "I was not going to hurt your boyfriend. I was just testing his courage. I could use a brave, broad-shouldered lad like him in my troop. Anyway, if he were a Pazzi, he would have wept and begged for his life." With a wave of a gauntleted hand, the boy was set free. "Your boyfriend must stay to do his work, but you should leave us. What we must do now may not be to a young girl's liking."

Enzo, seeing Placido stepping up behind Florentia, motioned for her to turn around. She took hold of her brother's wrist and rushed him down the hill, as the condottiere called Renato to him. "I like your spirit, lad. You don't scare easily. What is your name?" Renato answered, and the knight said, "Well, Renato, since your name means reborn, how would you like to be reborn as a soldier, instead of wasting away as a gravedigger on this dirt heap of an island? You see my men with their handsome uniforms and striking weapons— swords, spears, cudgels. With any one of them, you could separate a man's head from his shoulders, send it rolling, ear over ear, down the hill, and be honored for it. The ladies will bring out their special bag of tricks for you. Or maybe you've already been treated to every trick in the bag. No answer? All right then, I will leave you to your chosen profession, while I proceed with what I've had to come to this place to do because the mood in Florence has changed. All you hear now are pleas for amnesty, forgiveness. 'Have mercy!' 'No more bloodshed!' We're supposed to welcome the Pazzi traitors back from exile." He leaned over in the saddle, spat out his disdain, and said, "And now, to the business at hand."

From a shaded portico, soldiers sent a blindfolded man stumbling into the courtyard. His own tasseled sash, used to cover his eyes, could not hide the purple-black bruises adding color to his face, proof of the many kindnesses shown him by his captors. He wore a Turkish costume smeared with blood, some dried, some fresh and shining in the sun. Turning unseeing eyes toward a voice he had come to know all too well, the blindfolded man said, "I wish to make my last confession. Even you would not deny me that."

The condottiere shot back, "Do you take me for a godless heathen like those whose skirts you hid behind in Constantinople?" Shifting angry eyes to Enzo, he said, "Father, do your Christian duty." Enzo's ears must have heard those words, but his feet seemed unable to move. Then he managed to take a step toward the wagon.

"Where are you going, Your Eminence?"

Enzo stammered, "For the Last Rites, I will need—," indicating something to drape round his neck.

"Leave that."

"But when I hear Confession, I must wear—"

"I understand, Your Holiness. I said leave it. All you'll need to hear this sinner's confession is an ear."

Enzo stepped to the prisoner and began speaking in a solemn whisper. The man whispered in return, until the condottiere shouted, "That's enough chatter. Signor Baroncelli, are you fool enough to believe God will forgive you for stabbing a man as he bowed his head during Easter Mass? Nineteen stab wounds—"

"Not all nineteen. I was not alone."

"You struck the first blow! Deny it!"

"I do not deny it."

"Leave us, Father. Father, you may go. We won't need your services any longer. You may go, but the gravedigger boy stays. Didn't you hear me, Your Excellency? You may go. The Mass has ended. *Pax vobiscum.* Go in peace," said the condottiere, tracing the Sign of the Cross on the air with his sword. A soldier, leveling his spear, escorted the priest to the passageway, where Enzo turned to meet eyes with Renato. The boy signaled that he could take care of himself, and the black cassock stepped into the shadows and disappeared.

The prisoner spoke up again. "Whatever you are going to do to me, Sir, do it now."

"None of your false bravado here," barked the condottiere, and, rising in the saddle to appear more commanding, nodded to the hangman, a muscled man with no neck, who, careful not to disturb the prisoner's blindfold, slowly lowered the noose into place.

"Signor Bernardo Bandini de' Baroncelli," began the condottiere, "any final words or lofty sentiments we could pass on to your wife and bastard offspring?" The prisoner parted his lips to speak, and the executioner, as arranged, silenced his voice forever. The Black Death shifted in the saddle, patted the broad neck of his magnificent horse, and said to Renato, "You, too, could be riding a horse like this one day," and he reached down, offering to hoist the boy up. Renato made no move to accept the offered hand. After a silence, he said, "I have work to do, my chosen profession, as you called it."

The Black Death nodded, ordered his men to prepare to depart, then, leaning forward in the saddle, said to the boy, "I'm sorry to see you have chosen to spend your days digging paupers' graves until you fall into one yourself. Or maybe it is your girlfriend you can't drag yourself away from. I do not blame you. She is very beautiful. But, if you change your mind, there is more Pazzi hunting to do. Ser Jacopo's bastard has escaped me till now, but the reward money, recently tripled, is sure to be mine soon, to share with my men. Could a poor gravedigger-turned-soldier use a handful of gold coins to buy his sweetheart a pair of sapphire and emerald earrings to go with her eyes? Again, no answer? Well, wish me good hunting. My prey is so near I can smell him. My nostrils are quivering with the scent. Fare you well, gravedigger."

Entering the passageway, The Black Death rode serenely through the shadows, looking back and smiling as he called out to Renato, "Please kiss your girlfriend's eyes five or six times for me." He laughed, and the visor of his helmet dropped into place. His laugh echoed after him, and wave after wave of soldiers followed.

The courtyard was quiet for a time, then horse and rider returned to fling out a final command. "One more request, gravedigger. I want that Pazzi traitor buried standing up, so he will never be at rest. See to it."

The equestrian statue disappeared, leaving Renato to do the work of his chosen profession.

Chapter 3

The Mark of His Profession

R enato backed the wagon under the gently swaying man. Untying the fixed end of the rope, he said to him, "Constantinople must be an interesting place, but I plan to be going in a different direction very soon." When the man's feet touched the wagon, he dropped to his knees then onto his side.

Renato eased the wagon, weightier now, down the steep road, wading through the knee-high grass waving between the ruts.

In the cemetery there was one spot where he knew he must not dig, in the far corner where the Gibbet knelt each night, palms on the ground, forehead pressed to the dirt. The grave was unmarked, with not a stone to show that someone was buried there. The Gibbet knew who that someone was. The Childwoman knew, too. But they had vowed never to speak the name. Renato, forbidden to go near that sacred shrine, chose for Baroncelli's grave a spot on the opposite side of the cemetery.

With a spade and a shovel, into whose grain he had long ago pressed his blood, Renato prepared a place for Signor Baroncelli to rest, lying down, till Judgment Day.

While working, Renato was not thinking about the shortness of life. That thought would have needed more than his eighteen years to mature. His thoughts were of Florentia and how she had saved his life. She might not care about him the way he hoped, but at least she did not want him dead. A certain unstated, vague definiteness had developed between them over the last few summers. But one thing had not changed. She was of the rectory, and he was of the graveyard.

Renato had once asked Placido what he thought girls might like, what would please them. His friend answered that he did not know any girls, only his sister, but recalled reading in Boccaccio that girls like expensive jewelry. After considering further, Placido added, "But I'm sure any girl would like to be given a posy of flowers. Why do you ask?"

His friend's advice flowed through Renato's mind as he washed the graveyard dirt from his hands in the stream rippling beside the shack. He changed his shirt for one not much cleaner and made his way to the meadow swaying with wildflowers. Reaching for a blood-red poppy, he froze at the sight of his hand, for the stream could not wash away the mark of his profession—a black line of dirt buried under every fingernail. With the point of his pocket knife, he scraped and poked and dug and did not stop until every nail was the color of the poppy he hoped to give to Iride. Blood was reddening his knuckles. And then he saw her and fell face down in the dirt. Something had turned her eyes black, and, hurrying up the church steps, she scattered a congregation of chirruping sparrows, crying, "You came to church hoping to find Saint Francis? Well, you found me instead. I'll preach you a sermon, you sinners! You carry disease! You bathe in dirt! Go away! Go away and leave me alone!"

Chapter 4

The Beginner's Fee

R enato wandered off, not caring where his feet were taking him or whether the blade of the knife he flipped in the air landed point-first in the palm of his hand. He was working himself into the blackest and most satisfying of moods, in which he saw himself the hero of a tragedy so sad it could not be inflicted upon a weak-hearted public. So, it was after some hesitation that he allowed himself to smile at the sound of cheerful music wafting up from the seashore. His eyes ballooned at the vision of an impossibly tall man, with a squirrel on his shoulder, skipping before a line of music makers playing rainbow-ribboned instruments. A leaping little man was bang, bang, banging an undersized drum with an oversized spoon, while a high-stepping graybeard passed a saw across a fiddle that split apart then snapped back together. A barrel-chested fellow with a cascading mustache was tooting a toy horn whose church-sized bell blew iridescent bubbles that wobbled in the air and burst on the backside of a tambourine-jangling angel with bright yellow hair, who waved to Renato and called for him to come down from the bluff and join the fun. He shook his head. She pouted sweetly—how could he be so unfriendly and downright cruel? He shrugged. She, not taking "No" for an answer, started up the slope. Renato met her halfway, and they ran hand in hand to the others who surrounded Renato with smiling eyes—all but the barrel-chested fellow who looked daggers at the newcomer and said, each word puffing out his cascading mustache, "Have you come to kill us?"

"Kill you?"

"Yes, with that knife in your hand."

"Oh, this," said Renato, who no sooner pocketed his knife than the ruffian pulled out a knife of his own and stabbed Renato in the heart. Thoughts about the shortness of life instantly matured in Renato's mind, until the killer flopped the rubber blade of his weapon back and forth before the boy's eyes.

"I see you are glad to be alive," said the impossibly tall man, jumping down from stilts to a height that still tickled the clouds. "We, too, are glad to be alive, for a different reason."

The gray-bearded, white-eyebrowed leader of the troupe explained, "You see, we've just come from a ticklish situation in Florence, where power is changing hands, and not in a gentle way."

Troupe members took turns continuing the recitation:

"...We were in the center..."

"...of the courtyard ..."

"... of Palazzo Medici..."
"... in the middle of... "
"... Pulcinella's Romance... "
"... in our costumes and masks... "
"... when an anti-Medici mob... "
"... charged in, yelling... "
"... Liberty!..."
"... Liberty!..."
"... Liberty!..."
"... because the Medici... "
"... who are bankers..."
"... are being ousted... "
"... to be replaced by... "
"... the Pazzi..."
"... who are... "
"... guess what... "
"... also bankers... "
"... *Viva La Repubblica!*"

The genial graybeard, reclaiming his role as master of ceremonies, said, "I really thought we were all going to die." And the tall fellow, in comic tears, sobbed, "Yes, and right in the middle of my big love scene."

"But," concluded the graybeard, "we escaped and sailed away to play another day. And here we are, to do just that, on the island of Elba. So, all ended happily, as comedies should. Let me introduce myself. I am Signor Pantalone, and we are *I Comici di Napoli* of the Commedia dell'Arte. And your name, good Sir?"

"My name is Renato. But, Signor Pantalone, you must have lost your way in the fog. You are not on the island of Elba. You are on Pianosa Island. There is nothing here but a cemetery, a church, and a prison."

"A cemetery, a church, and a prison. Three institutions from which we have, so far, escaped. Therefore, we shall set sail, first thing in the morning. Now, young man, is there an inn nearby?"

"No. I'm afraid there is only a cemetery, a church, and a—"

"Stop right there. Well, we are used to not having a roof over our heads. We'll set up our tent in the next cove and be on our way after sunrise. I see you have taken an interest in my bride, the fair Colombina."

"Well, I have never seen hair that color before."

The barrel-chested fellow leaned in to say, "It doesn't seem real, does it?" And, in a stage whisper, "The long hairs are yellow, but if you look closely, all the short hairs down below are black."

Renato said, "Oh, yes, I see that."

"Brighella, you are a beast," snapped Colombina, drawing her arm back to deliver a slap. Brighella ducked, and Renato rubbed his cheek.

"You should have ducked," said Brighella. Colombina cocked her arm again, Brighella ducked, so did Renato, and the slap passed harmlessly over the head of the very little man.

"You ducked, Renato. Good," said Brighella. "You learn fast. Would you like to join our troupe?"

"Stop it," said Colombina. "The boy might believe you."

Renato said, "I would be glad to join you, that is, if you sail to the New World."

"If we sail to the New World?" said Brighella. "It just so happens that the New World is our next stop, after Elba."

"I could play the part of Pulcinella," offered Renato. "My father often calls me Pulcinella."

"My God, he's perfect!" cried Brighella. "Quick, someone run and grab a costume from the boat."

Moments later, a flurry of attending hands drew back to reveal the eager young novice in a black mask with a nose like a lump of coal, floppy cone hat with pompom dangling, and ridiculously oversized blouse and pants, white to match the hat.

The upstandingly tall man, bending over to half his height laughing, howled, "He looks like a blackbird lost in a white cloud!" While beneath him, the little man, leaning back with laughter, chuckled, "No, no. I'd say a blackberry dropped in a bowl of cream!"

"Our new Pulcinella was born to be a clown," said Brighella, "but let's see if he can dance. Pulcinella must dance with the grace of a ballerina. Dance for us, Pulcinella! Dance!"

Hearing laughter and applause and hoping with a beating heart to win the right to join his new friends on their voyage to the New World—in a hat whose bouncing pompom found its way into his mouth—dizzy behind a mask through which he saw nothing but his lump-of-coal nose—tripped up by sleeves and pant legs twice the length of his limbs—Renato-Pulcinella flailed about in a whirl of twirls and leaps that would have fractured every leg he had, had the kindly graybeard not stepped in to break the boy's fall.

"That's enough now," said Signor Pantalone. "Leave the poor boy alone. Go, you fools, and set up our tent for the night. We sail after sunrise."

Colombina helped Renato out of the Pulcinella costume she carried away, except for the black mask Renato asked to hold a while longer. Signor Pantalone sat the boy down beside him on a flat rock jutting out from the slope. Smiling to see Renato holding the mask by its nose, he said, "You know, son, you say you would like to join our troupe. And I understand. I do. But ours is not the carefree life you might imagine it to be. We wander from place to place, never knowing whether we'll be lionized or have the dogs set on us. Many a night there's only a tree branch between us and a storm, and precious little to eat. No, believe me, son, you are better off here on this island with parents who love you."

Signor Pantalone stood up, held out an open palm, and Renato watched the lump of coal leave his fingers. "I see you have a farmer's hands," said the good man, adding as he walked away, "Farming is a noble profession."

Renato was staring at his fingernails when Brighella sat beside him. "Listen to the old man, Renato. He's trying to do you a favor. Anyway, you probably don't have the money for the beginner's fee. You see, we'd have to clothe you, feed you, buy you costumes, pay your travel expenses. All that costs money."

"But I have money," said Renato, reaching into his pocket and placing a coin in Brighella's hand.

"One florin?" said Brighella, flipping the coin over in his palm. "It would take more than one florin."

"That's not a florin. That's an ancient Roman coin. There's an emperor on one side and a half-naked goddess on the other," said Renato, rising with the coin now in his hand.

"Where are you going?"

"To show Signor Pantalone I have the beginner's fee."

"No, no, no, no, no, no, no. Don't do that," said Brighella, placing a hand on Renato's shoulder. "You see, it's not about the money with the old man. He'd be insulted. Let me talk to him for you. Come back tomorrow morning. I'll have it all arranged."

"I don't know," said Renato, holding so tight to the coin he could tell the goddess from the emperor.

Colombina called out, "Handsome, we need your muscles," and Brighella separated the coin from Renato's hand. "Let me handle this for you," he said. "Remember, the New World is our next stop."

"After Elba," corrected the boy.

"After Elba, yes, of course."

Colombina swayed close to Renato, cooing, "Too bad you won't be coming with us."

"But I will. I have the beginner's fee."

"The?"

"Beginner's fee," said Renato, looking to Brighella. "He's going to talk to Signor Pantalone for me."

Brighella opened his palm, and Colombina opened her eyes. "I think that Brighella and I, both, should talk to Signor Pantalone," she said. Touching the boy's cheek, she breathed, "I didn't hurt you before, with that slap, did I?"

"Didn't even feel it," he said.

"Till tomorrow then," said the angel who spread her wings and flew away.

"Till tomorrow," said Brighella.

"And please," said Renato, "when you talk to Signor Pantalone, tell him I have two friends who must come with me, or I take back the coin."

"Of course," said Brighella. "Bring your two friends along. That would be splendid, Pulcinella, splendid."

God's Greatest Blessing

Three times Renato knocked on the rectory door, and three times Enzo sent him away, saying first that Placido and Florentia were finishing their dinner. Later, he claimed they had to clean up after their meal. Then it was their Bible lesson.

Renato, knowing he would be leaving the island early next morning and wanting to say goodbye to his father, found the Gibbet on his knees at the unmarked grave. Not wanting to disturb his father's nightly vigil, Renato made his way to the cemetery shack where the Childwoman lay awake with the crucifix pressed to her lips. Renato whispered, "Mother, I have something to tell you. I am leaving tomorrow morning for the New World."

The Childwoman placed the crucifix close to her head on the pillow, her white hair aging the figure on the cross. "My son, you would leave for the New World just when your mother is about to leave this one?"

"You will be here when I return someday to bring you back with me."

"The Lord has seen to it that you have no boat to take you from me, so you will not be leaving."

"But I found a valuable coin worth enough to pay my way and good people kind enough to take me with them."

"Let me see the coin. Put it here on the pillow next to the cross."

"I don't have it with me now."

"So, it is an imaginary coin. They are the most valuable of all."

"It's a real coin. A Roman coin. I found it under some flooring stones in the charnel house and gave it to Brighella to pay Signor Pantalone—"

"Pantalone?"

"—the beginner's fee."

"Beginner's fee?"

"Yes, they have a boat. And tomorrow morning—"

The Childwoman closed the blue-veined bones of her hand around Renato's wrist and said, "This island has driven you mad, like the rest of us. There is no coin. There is no Signor Pantalone, no boat to take you to the New World. You will see I am telling the truth. Go now, and sleep. Sleep is taking hold of me right now. At least, I think it's sleep. Go. Sleep. Sleep is God's greatest blessing, after death."

Call Me Amerigo

But Renato could not sleep and next morning before sunrise he was at the tree that angled up beside the rectory, tossing pebbles at Placido's window. With each toss, the pebble struck harder, then grew larger, until the window opened reluctantly and a sleepy face appeared. "Renato, my friend, are you crazy or just unforgivably cruel?"

"Placido, get dressed, run upstairs, wake your sister, and both of you come with me. I paid Signor Pantalone the beginner's fee with a Roman coin, and he's going to take the three of us to the New World."

"You are dreaming, and I am sleeping," yawned Placido, pulling the window shut with a bang.

A window swung open on the floor above, brushing against the leaves of the tree just outside. Florentia's face popped out, framed by the green leaves all around her. "I heard what you just told Placido. You are as crazy as ever, Renato."

"Call me Amerigo this morning, because the three of us are leaving this island for the New World. You remember the other night, in the charnel house, I told you about finding a Roman coin that was going to pay our way there?" Florentia did not remember any such thing, never having been in the charnel house. But because Renato's adventures, though often proving misadventures, were always good for a lark, and since Florentia was as skilled as the boys at tree climbing and tree descending, the three friends were soon racing for the shore, now one, now another, in the lead.

Placido, panting, called out, in spurts, "I can't wait to see that Roman coin. It must be a gold aureus with Augustus on the front face and Venus on the back face."

Amerigo, sprinting to the lead, said, "I don't know about her back face, but Venus must have just stepped out of the bathtub, because she's holding a bar of soap, and the towel has slipped completely off her backside."

"Ha! That's the Callipygian Venus!"

"Which Venus?" asked Florentia, taking the lead, then losing it to Placido who laughed, "Venus of the Lovely Buttocks! What Amerigo's calling a bar of soap must be the Golden Apple awarded her by Paris, Prince of Troy."

There was no time for Placido to explain the Judgment of Paris or the Apple of the Hesperides, for the sun shot up into the sky like a firework, spreading its warming rays over the meadow, the bluff, and the seashore, where the three friends now stood staring at their old enemy the horizon. There were no musicians, no impossibly tall man, no yellow-haired angel, no Roman coin, no boat to carry them to the New World.

There was, instead, standing above them, Enzo the Raven glowering down from his perch at the edge of the bluff. He ordered his two wards back to the rectory to prepare breakfast. Florentia started up the slope, and Placido followed, leaving The Dreamer alone to stare at the empty horizon.

Florentia did not return to the rectory. She drifted to the meadow where she lay among poppies leaning into her vision of clouds reshaping themselves on a field of blue. Mere wisps massed into a mountain dividing into two peaks with a valley between where a blue lake opened only to dry up again. Then the mountain disappeared, and in its place came the dome of a church that puffed up until it was the magnificent cathedral of Florence where her wedding would take place.

Florentia rose to her feet, picked the reddest poppy, and headed for the rectory. Arriving at the church steps, alive with chirruping sparrows, Florentia bent down to ask if they were angry with her for being so mean to them the other day. On bended knee she begged them to forgive her. The birds, deciding in her favor, gathered at her feet. Florentia, hearing Enzo calling her, rose up, and her little friends rose up, too.

Entering the rectory, she tiptoed past the study and Enzo's voice, bounded up the stairs to her room, closed the door, leaned back with the poppy in her hand, and gave a little scream. Renato was standing at the open window.

"What are you doing here?"

"I don't know," he explained.

"You really are out of your mind, aren't you?"

"Yes," he said.

"Enzo will come looking for me. You have to leave." She pressed her ear to the door. "He's coming up the stairs." Renato did not move. Florentia, rushing to the window, opened it further. Renato did not move. A knock at the door. Enzo's voice—"Are you all right? I thought I heard a scream."

"I saw a mouse."

"A mouse?"

"No, a bee. But I opened the window, and he flew out." Florentia, eyeing her unexpected visitor, brought her face to his, mouthing, "Out." But before she could close her lips around the word, Renato parted them with a kiss. She said, "Ummm, bees make nice honey. Tastes good." Kissing him quickly twice, she whispered, "Now, fly," and eased him closer to the window. The doorknob turned, and Enzo stepped in, saying, "What's this about a bee?"

No bee ever flew across the meadow as fast as Renato on the wings of that kiss. He was rushing past the stream beside the cemetery shack when he heard his mother say, "Where are you going in such a hurry?"

"I have work to do in the graveyard."

The Childwoman, washing clothes at the stream, said, "I'm doing my work. You better hurry to yours. It's going to rain. Are you digging a grave for me? My day is almost here. I can taste the dirt on my tongue." And she went back to scrubbing the threadbare smock she hoped to wear to paradise.

Renato knelt beside her. She said, "This stream pushes harder every year." Looking up from her work, she passed the bones of her hand lightly over his face, as a blind person might do, and said, "My son, that priest came to the shack a while back but not to minister to me. He'll come later for that and bring his wooden box with the black cross. He came to talk about you. He told me you've been looking in a sinful way at the red-haired girl. 'With sin in his heart,' he said. He's the kind of priest who sees sin everywhere but in the mirror. He's supposed to be like Jesus to us. That man, like Jesus? Jesus must be turning in his grave." Renato steadied his mother's hand against the onrushing stream. The water was cold. "Listen to me," said the Childwoman. "The priest told me he has a plan for that girl's future. He says she is his ward. I say she is his prisoner, because a plan can be a prison. The future can be a prison. Do you understand me? Do you understand what your mother is telling you?"

Renato nodded but he did not understand.

Florentia and the Pazzi Boy

Part Two: "I'm never leaving this coffin"

Chapter 5

"I Am the Pazzi Boy"

F lorentia, tired of trying to sleep, rolled out of bed and partially filled her completely empty hope chest by sitting inside and hugging her knees. Lulled by the sound of rain pinging off the leaves outside, she closed her eyes and, when she opened them, saw Renato climb in through the window and refuse to leave, and when she tried to tell him he really must leave, he kissed her. Lightning chased him away. Distant thunder turned into the rumble of advancing male voices, and bouncing points of light, seen through the rain, became the flames of approaching torches.

Quickly into her robe and out to the landing, Florentia stepped back as Enzo rushed down the stairs to a thundering pounding at the door.

Placido, bounding up from his room, begged Florentia not to let those men take him away.

"Nobody's going to take you away. Enzo is talking to two men at the door. Why should anyone want to take you away?"

"You know why," said Placido. Florentia made no reply but drew her brother from the landing to just inside her room where they peeked around the doorjamb at Enzo escorting the two visitors to his study. Florentia and Placido recognized the stout fellow as the man who docked once a month with food and supplies donated by a charity in Florence. Because of his drooping eyelid, Placido had nicknamed him Half Mast. The other fellow, fashionably dressed, animated in his manner, must be a man of some consequence, at least in his own mind, for as he spoke he handed his rain-dripping head covering to Half Mast with an air of inflated self-importance not deflated by a facial tic that caused his bushy black eyebrows to arch their backs like two caterpillars inching across his forehead.

Florentia and Placido knew they ought not to smile, aware of how much terrible pain, anguish, and suffering those ridiculous eyebrows must cause the poor fellow. The caterpillars rested, and the gentleman lifted his gaze to the upstairs doorway where two young faces at the doorjamb, one above the other, smiled down at him. Enzo, pointing upstairs, whispered something to the gentleman who nodded and stepped into the study. Enzo paused to aim a Do Not Disturb stare at his wards before entering the study and pulling the door shut tight.

"You see," said Florentia, "there was nothing to be afraid of. That was actually rather amusing."

"Yes, I'm smiling now," said Placido, "but when I saw the torches, I thought it was The Black Death coming to cut me into nineteen pieces."

"It's just someone from the charity come to talk to Enzo. Actually, dear brother, you may as well know the real reason that gentleman is here. He's here to paint my portrait, the way they do when a faraway king wants to see what his future bride looks like."

"My dear sister, let me tell you the real reason that man is here. As The Black Death told Renato, the Pazzi clan is returning from exile. That gentleman was sent by my true family to take me back with him—because I am the Pazzi boy."

"You were, are, and will forever be, like me, the orphan child of a humble prison guard and a housekeeper at this rectory. Now, you stay here. I'm going downstairs to listen at the door."

Florentia, creeping one stair at a time, heard only the sound of her footsteps and the rise and fall of male voices, until she arrived at the study door and pressed her blue eye to the keyhole. The well-dressed fellow must be a matchmaker for one of the richest families of Florence, because Enzo did not scold him when he plopped himself down in Enzo's favorite chair with the lion-paw armrests. Enzo did not say a thing when the man leaned his rain-slicked hair against the Do Not Touch painting of the Madonna and Child.

"I want to see, too!" hissed Placido, and the two siblings butted heads until the harder head claimed victory.

"He's talking about a dowry for me, isn't he?" said Florentia.

"No. I'll tell you what he's saying in a second."

"It's about painting my portrait, isn't it?"

Placido, his eyeball taking the shape of the keyhole, gave this account: "Lorenzo de' Medici died two years ago. His son Piero, who succeeded him, threw open the gates of the city to the invading French king, because—"

"My turn," announced Florentia. Placido sat back on his heels, rubbed his eye, and listened to his sister say: "Learning that Piero surrendered to the French king in exchange for titles of nobility for the Medici, the people of Florence ousted that traitor who was lucky to escape with his life. With the Medici gone, the Pazzi are free to return from Paris."

"I told you so," said Placido, who returned to the keyhole to witness the gentleman placing a velvet drawstring pouch in Enzo's open palm.

"That's my dowry money," said Florentia, pressing her green eye, this time, to the keyhole. She saw the gentleman with the active eyebrows tell Enzo, "You'll find this payment a good deal more generous than the monthly installment, to demonstrate the Pazzi family's gratitude that you not only saved the child from certain death in Florence but tutored him here, over the years, to undertake his role as heir to a great fortune. The lad looks to be in excellent health. By the way, has he read all these books?"

"That boy," answered Enzo, "knows more about Roman history than his own."

"Of course, you haven't yet told him his true identity, but the moment is coming when you should be clear and open with the boy. The joyful family reunion will take place very soon. Till then, be on your guard. Medici agents have tripled the reward money. Trust no one."

Half Mast moved quickly to the door. The doorknob turned. The door swung open, and the gentleman saw the two young spies standing so stiff it seemed they were hoping to pass for statues and go unnoticed.

"You must be the two orphans we of the Confraternity have been supporting these many years. So glad to meet you both. Let me say—"

Suddenly, the rectory door banged open, and a rock-faced man, his lip cut and bleeding, shoved Renato to the middle of the room. "I found this one hanging around outside the window. It took three of us to settle him down."

The gentleman said, "And who might this young man be?"

Renato was about to answer, when Enzo stepped in with, "A local boy."

"Please, Father, I'm sure the young man can speak for himself."

"Of course," said Enzo, becoming aware, as he stepped back, that the too-many buttons of his cassock were out of alignment.

"Well, young fellow," said the gentleman, "what have you got to say for yourself, bloodying the lip of one of my guards?"

"I was worried about my friends," said Renato.

"But I mean your friends no harm."

"I see that now, Sir. And I am sorry."

Enzo said, "Renato, this gentleman is from the Confraternity of Saint Francis, which is—"

"Thank you, Father. I will explain. Our charity is dedicated to providing for every orphan in Florentine territory. Is this boy an orphan, Father? You never told us about him."

"He is not an orphan. He is my son," said the Gibbet, bent forward in the doorway. "Renato, your mother has been asking for you." Pointing to Enzo with his cane, the Gibbet added, "We will be needing your services in the cemetery shack very soon. Make sure you bring the box with the black cross."

Renato, glancing back at his friends, followed his father into the night.

Lamentation

Enzo and Florentia walked the visitors to the pier and stood side by side as the ship got underway.

It was not until the ship sank beneath the horizon that Florentia reminded herself she was not actually aboard that vessel bound for the city her mother used to say was named after her. She heard the rain before she saw it pinging off her upturned palm, and realized that Enzo was no longer standing beside her. She caught up with him as he was leaving the church with the wooden box under his arm. She stepped into his path. He walked past her without speaking. Florentia stepped in front of him and, walking backwards, said, simply, "Well?"

"I cannot talk now. You see that," he told her, his face as grim as the rite he was on his way to perform.

"Foolish me," she said. "I was sure that the gentleman from Florence came here to paint my portrait." Stumbling on the rain-slick pebbles of the path, she reached for his arm.

"Careful. You'll make me drop this box. Leave me to my work."

The rain falling in a broad chessboard pattern over the island, Enzo entered a black square and quickened his steps. Florentia kept pace. "Tell me what you and the gentleman with the caterpillar eyebrows talked about, and I'll leave you alone."

"The gentleman has a name. Signor Farfalla."

"Signor Butterfly. I like that. And what did Signor Butterfly say?"

"You know very well what he said. You were listening at the door."

"I missed the first part, where you talked about arranging a match for me. But I did see him put a draw-string pouch with my dowry money in your hand."

"We can talk about that later," said Enzo, holding out the wooden box to remind her what he was on his way to do.

"You won't need that box or the holy oil or a crucifix, because the Childwoman is not going to die. No one's ever going to die again, because you kept your promise, and there's going to be a wedding. Tell me you kept your promise." The cemetery shack came into view. Florentia stayed back, then ran after Enzo, shouting through the rain, "You didn't talk to him about me at all, did you?" She grabbed his arm. The box fell but did not break. Florentia reached down. Enzo pushed her hand away. Rising with the box in his hand, he said, "The old woman is dying in that shack, and all you can think about is yourself." Starting down the muddy path to the shack, he told her, "Go home now. Do as I tell you."

.   .   .

The Gibbet, knowing the priest was standing at the open door, turned with a mix of gratitude and dread. He showed Enzo to an oft-repaired chair beside the bed, where the Childwoman seemed to be in need of the Last Sacrament, her skull pressing through the last transparent layer of skin.

Renato was on his knees stroking the blue veins of his mother's hand. Enzo set the wooden box on the bed and reached in to remove a crucifix. The boy motioned toward the crucifix on the wall near his mother's pillow. The cassock's black sleeve passed across the Childwoman's face like a shadow, and she split her dry lips enough to say, "No, Father. This is not the time. When my time comes, I will send for you." And, with the slightest movement of eyes sunken deep in her skull, she let the priest know he could leave.

The Truth Revealed

Enzo had almost reached the rectory when a pebble, grazing his ear, landed on the path ahead of him. A second pebble bounced off the wooden box in his hand. Speaking into the darkness, he said, "You were right about the old woman. She is not dying, at least not yet."

A few steps later, a pebble glanced off his shoulder. "You try my patience," he said and walked on unmolested until he entered the church. Hearing footsteps echoing behind him, he turned and said, "Think about where you are right now."

"I think I know for the first time just where I am," said Florentia and, with her last pebble, took aim at The Raven's black heart and hit the target. The Raven flew to the altar, Florentia shouting after him, "Where is the husband you promised me? The velvet pouch that Signor Farfalla put in your hand isn't my dowry money at all, is it?" Enzo, turning at the sacristy door, whispered, "Lower your voice, or Placido will hear you in the rectory." Florentia screamed, "I don't care," and pursued him through the sacristy, across to the rectory, and into his study, where Enzo turned on her. "Be patient. Things are changing in Florence, just as I told you they would."

"You lied to me."

"At the proper time, I will see that a match is arranged that will make you a fine lady of Florence, just as I promised."

"I am going to die on this island—on this abandoned ant hill."

Enzo, seated in the lion-paw chair beneath the Madonna and Child, said, "You are not going to die on this island."

Florentia selected a book from the bookcase, put it back in place, and said, "The next time Signor Farfalla comes to this ant hill, I want you, right here in this room, with me present, to tell him to start making arrangements for my wedding in Florence, or I will tell Renato the truth about who he is and make him my rich husband."

"But I am the Pazzi boy," said Placido leaning against the doorjamb with arms crossed. "I never knew my mother. My father, who died before I was born, was not a prison guard. He was Jacopo de' Pazzi."

"My dear brother, Enzo can tell you, I was not quite three years old but I was there the morning the Childwoman brought you into this world."

"The Childwoman is my mother?"

"The Childwoman helped deliver you into this world."

"If I am not the Pazzi boy, then why did you both stop me from going to the prison courtyard that day? But I know why. You did it to protect me, the Pazzi boy, from The Black Death."

Florentia looked to Enzo who looked away. "All right," she said, "I'll be the first to confess. Placido, I have been guilty of going along with Enzo's scheme to cover his blunders by passing you off as the Pazzi boy, blunders that began long before he came to this island."

"Florentia, stop!" said Enzo, bringing his palm down hard on the lion's paw.

"No, I won't stop. My brother must finally be told about a certain clergyman caught selling, to wealthy Florentine ladies, forged grants of Papal forgiveness that supposedly canceled centuries of future suffering in purgatory. But his biggest blunder was keeping every golden florin for himself, instead of rolling them down the road to Rome. The Pope ordered him defrocked, out of the priesthood, and sentenced him to do penance on this godforsaken island as his purgatory on earth."

Placido turned disbelieving eyes to his tutor. "Defrocked means you're not allowed to administer the sacraments. But you've been doing that all along. You heard Baroncelli's confession in the prison courtyard. You promised the Gibbet you would perform the Last Rites at the cemetery shack."

Enzo, straightening the Madonna and Child, said, "If what I do offers solace and comfort to those in need...."

Placido stepped to the bookcase where Enzo had guided him in his studies, reached for the top row of books, and knocked them, one after another, to the floor.

Florentia, after the last book had landed at her feet, said, "Placido, there's more to tell."

"That's enough," demanded Enzo.

"No," said Placido, "I will hear the full confession."

Picking up the book at her feet, Florentia continued, "Enzo brought the Pazzi baby here thinking the housekeeper at the rectory, your mother and mine, would nurse and care for the child. But she passed away soon after Enzo arrived, so he turned to the caretaker couple at the cemetery. With the prison shut down because of the plague, they were about to leave the island, but Enzo persuaded them to stay."

"They didn't need much persuading," said Enzo. "They had no place to go and no money to get there."

"And so," said Florentia, "the heir to the Pazzi fortune grew up a gravedigger, and, since Half Mast, on his monthly supply visits, took for granted that you, brought up around books and paintings, were the Pazzi boy, Enzo let him go on reporting that to the charity."

"This entire tangle will soon be unraveled," said Enzo, "to everyone's satisfaction."

"To everyone's satisfaction?" said Florentia.

"Yes. You will become a proud signora of Florence, and you, Placido, will take over as lord of Palazzo Pazzi, with all the books and paintings and Roman works of art your heart desires."

Placido noticed a book that had fallen open to a woodcut of a beautifully handsome Botticelli angel silently strumming a stringed instrument. The book had opened to that page because Placido had turned to it, in admiration, many times before. Florentia was saying, "Now, Enzo, tell my brother what you believe the future holds for you."

"I am confident," said Enzo, "that the Pazzi family will use its influence with the Vatican to reward my many years of service by having the Pope's own fingers place an archbishop's miter on my head. It's not so unheard of."

Placido, looking up from the handsome Botticelli angel in the woodcut, said, "And what's to become of Renato?"

"Nothing needs to become of Renato," said Enzo. "He is fine as he is. In any case, Renato is not prepared for life in Florence. You are."

"That is true," said Placido. Then he set about collecting and returning every book to its proper place. Only one book remained, the one Florentia still held in her hand. As he slipped the book from her fingers, she said, "Placido, my brother. My brother. My brother. Renato is your friend. Would you take the place that belongs to him?"

Placido left the bookcase and stood beside Enzo seated under the protection of the Madonna and Child.

Florentia said, "Oh, how I hate this, how I hate you both, how I hate myself," and ran crying from the room.

Placido, after waiting to hear the flurry of footsteps on the stairs and the bang of an upstairs door, turned to Enzo and said, "But I would not be taking Renato's place because, despite what she says, I still believe I am the Pazzi boy. Tell me. Am I the Pazzi boy?"

Enzo answered, "Yes, you are."

"Then she is not my sister."

Enzo replied, "No, she is not."

Placido returned to the bookcase to make certain he had placed every book in its proper, chronological sequence.

Enzo, observing the boy a while, remarked, "Placido, don't you think Petrarch should come before Boccaccio and Dante before Petrarch?"

Chapter 6

"I Am Not the Pazzi Boy"

N ext morning, Placido, sitting cross-legged at the end of the pier, was cross-examining his conscience. Staring down at the choppy water, his thoughts rose and fell, never coming to rest. Trying to separate Right from Wrong was like separating salt from pepper piled in a heap. He was finally making some progress awakening a sense of Right when his left foot fell asleep.

Limping around in a circle to shake off the numbness, Placido noticed Florentia bent over her planting in the vegetable garden and he said to the seagulls circling right over his head like the devil's halo, "She has always been a good sister to me, even though she is not my sister. I will reward her after I have made my triumphant entry into Florence, with barefoot children tossing rose petals at my feet. Once I have settled into my role as head of the Pazzi banking empire, I will see that a suitable match is made for her, though not, of course, into a noble family, such as my own. After all, she is from humble stock."

Placido also considered how he might best use his vast wealth to benefit his childhood friend

Renato and thought of purchasing for him a collection of rare Roman coins or, perhaps, a cemetery of his own in Florence, far outside the city walls.

Those thoughts, so beneath him, came under attack from above, when the circling seagulls, shrieking and squawking, took turns swooping dangerously close to Placido's conscience. "Yellow-beaked Furies!" he yelled, as his attackers chased him limping and ducking to the end of the pier before flying off, leaving the boy trembling from head to left foot.

. . .

In the graveyard high on the hill, Renato's shovel was carving a windowless, earth-walled room that did not need to be nearly as long or as deep as others. The boy's heart was not in his work, and he raised his eyes to a passing formation of birds pointing him down the hill. He followed their flight until they slowed to fluttering specks settling, in twos and threes, in the vegetable garden.

Renato tossed his shovel aside.

. . .

"I'm pretty good with a spade myself," said Renato.

"Yes, I know," said Florentia, continuing her planting.

"We're going to get soaked in a minute," he said, eyeing an arriving flotilla of rain clouds.

"Yes, I know," said Florentia, reaching for a handful of onion bulbs.

"Funny," he said, "we both bury things, but the ones I bury don't come up again."

"They will if you wait long enough."

"Can I help you?" he said.

Smiling, she placed three onion bulbs in his open palm, and he got to work.

"Not that way," she said gently. "You don't lay the bulb down like a dead person. You want to put it in standing up. No, don't bury it completely. Just partway. Yes, like that. When you slow down, I can see you have good hands."

Then Renato noticed something about Florentia that made her even more beautiful in his eyes. She had dark dirt lines under her fingernails.

"Are you angry with me for climbing in through your window?"

A sudden downpour changed her answer to, "Let's hurry!"

"Your onions!"

"We'll plant more!"

They were running hand in hand, Florentia crying out, "Where are we going?"

"I know the perfect place," he said.

And they dashed across the meadow, laughing with the childlike delight of running full speed through the rain. The harder they ran, the harder the rain fell, and the harder the rain fell, the harder they ran. "It's just a drizzle!" Renato shouted.

"A fine mist!" yelled Florentia, slowing to a stop and adding, "I need to catch my breath." But as he slowed down, she ran off laughing, "I'll get there first. Oh, I see now where we're headed. The hollow tree. Wonderful!"

They reached the hollow tree together, hands on knees, heads down, hair dripping past mouths breathing heavily, rain-soaked clothes clinging to their bodies, eyes meeting. Florentia ducked under the A-shaped opening first, and inside they snuggled together on a floor of dry leaves, listening for the raindrop music tinkling like chimes.

The hollow tree was where the friends used to play children's games. There was more room inside then. Now it was necessary to stay close together.

. . .

The rain had continued on its way. The sun now ruled the sky. Renato peeked from the A-shaped opening of the hollow tree, reached back, and he and Florentia stepped out. She threw her arms out wide to embrace the sun then let out a shriek and ran through the meadow, twirling and singing out, "Iride," the word for rainbow, which happened to be Renato's private name for her.

"Iride, Iride, Iride, I love you, Iride," she cried, celebrating the splendiferous ribbon of color arcing high over the meadow and touching down in the sea. Renato joined in, chanting, "Iride, Iride, Iride, I love you, Iride," and they danced round and round beneath the rainbow until they dropped in a heap of arms and legs.

Renato jumped to his feet, pointing out to sea at two dolphins leaping out of the water. Florentia rose up, clapped her hands with joy, and threw her arms around Renato. Seeing Placido at the rectory door, she waved and called out, "Look! Dolphins! Aren't they wonderful! There they go again, jumping clear out of the water! They love the rainbow, too! They're leaping in an arc to make the same shape!"

Placido yelled, "Enzo wants you inside!" Florentia gave Renato a quick kiss in parting. "Goodbye. Thank you. The hollow tree was wonderful. I hope it rains again soon."

At the rectory door, she said to her brother, "Didn't you love the dolphins?"

"I didn't see them," he said.

"Two leaping dolphins, like the ones on the Pazzi family crest. Renato was the first to see them—and you didn't see them at all," she said with a tilt of her head and stepped into the rectory.

Placido looked out to sea but he saw only the horizon.

. . .

Placido, to unlock the mystery of Renato's birth, and his own, would not trust the word of a person who might or might not be his sister—nor that of a defrocked priest. Having earned his nickname The Professor by always going to the pages of a book for answers, Placido made his way to the study, believing the book that would solve the riddle of his past was locked away in Enzo's desk drawer.

Entering Enzo's study, Placido's gaze rested on the Madonna and Child. He had seen that painting many times before, but this time a singular detail caught his eye—the baby on his mother's lap was pointing to an open book. The message was clear: "The book you seek will unlock the secret of your birth. Find that book and read your destiny." Placido touched palms with the baby in the painting then stepped to Enzo's desk, eyeing the locked drawer. With a few twists of his pocket knife, the drawer slid open. He pulled out the topmost book, blew the dust from the cover, laid it on the desk, opened it slowly, and heard a voice say, "So, you didn't take my word for it."

Enzo reached past Placido's shoulder, pulled a timeworn ledger from the drawer, and set it on the desk. "Here's the book you want. Go ahead. Open it. All the baptismal records are there. Let me help you," he said and turned page after page. Placido ran his fingers down the entries. Coming to the final page, he gazed up at Enzo. "It's missing.

The important page is missing. There is nothing but a jagged edge."

"Yes, someone tore that page out," said Enzo. "I did."

Placido said, "Show it to me. If what you say is true, and I am the Pazzi boy, show me that page. Or I will go to Renato myself and tell him the truth." Enzo turned to the Madonna and Child, pulled it down from the wall, leaned it against the desk, and held out an open palm. "The knife, please."

With Placido's knife, Enzo scraped away at the brick below the nail that had held the painting in place. Finally able to slide the brick out from the wall, Enzo reached into the opening, took out a folded piece of paper, brushed it off, and handed it to Placido who laid it beside the jagged edge in the ledger. The two fit together perfectly.

Placido began studying the birth entries for dates and names. Years of water damage had caused many words to trail off into unreadable smudges. Still, Placido was able to find entries for himself and for Renato. But there was no entry with the name Pazzi. There was, though, an entry for a child baptized during that same period. The child's given name could easily be read. The name was Emiliano. Placido looked up from the page. He had never heard the name Emiliano spoken on Pianosa.

Enzo removed the jagged page from Placido's hand, folded it, returned it to the wall, replaced the brick, and set the Madonna and Child back on its nail. He returned the two ledgers, locked the drawer, and said to Placido, "What your sister told you—"

"My sister?"

"Yes, your sister. What Florentia told you was true, to a point. It is true that I brought the Pazzi baby here, as the family instructed me to do. It was a miracle the infant survived the journey from Florence, but the poor creature passed away on this island before he could take his first steps. I did not report that misfortune to Signora Pazzi because I believed in my heart that her heart could not bear the shock. Hadn't she suffered enough? For you now to take the place of the child she is longing to embrace would be an act of love and compassion."

Placido said, "So, I am not the Pazzi boy."

"No, you are not."

"But then, neither is Renato."

"That's right," said Enzo. "Neither is Renato."

Chapter 7

A Lock of Her Hair

F lorentia might be asleep at such a late hour, but there was nothing to stop Renato from finding a comfortable spot to sit between the dragon-tail roots of the tree angling up past her window.

Enzo, meanwhile, was standing outside Florentia's door. He turned the knob, took one step into the darkness, and waited for the click of the door closing behind him. He whispered her name. No answer. Moonlight beaming in through the open window whitened a corner of the bed. Enzo stepped closer and again whispered her name.

"I'm here," said her voice coming not from the bed but from the open hope chest by the window. Her hand rose up, and something heavy dropped onto the floor. Enzo picked it up—a pair of scissors—and said, "Why are you crying?"

Her voice answered, "I put on my mother's tattered wedding dress and sat down here. It isn't a wedding dress. It's just a dress she wore. I don't think they were ever actually married."

"You sat in your hope chest and you…?"

"…cut off all my hair."

"Come up out of there, and let me see you."

"No, never."

"But this morning, dancing with Renato under the rainbow, you seemed so happy."

"Yes, I was happy. I am happy. That's why I'm crying."

"I don't understand."

"Of course not. You're a man."

"Please come out of there."

"I am never leaving this coffin. I plan to rot here. Go away and leave me to rot in peace." Florentia's hand pulled the coffin lid shut.

Enzo, his eyes accustomed to the darkness, reached down to the floor and came up holding a lock of Florentia's hair. "All right, I'll go," he said and walked to the door. With the doorknob in his hand, he turned to say, "I think you should know that I did speak to Signor Farfalla about a match that would make you a lady of Florence. But that is so much water under the Ponte Vecchio now that you are determined to rot here."

The lid of the coffin rose up, slowly. Florentia's head appeared, then sank back down.

"A pity," said Enzo, "because it's all been arranged. The bravest young gallants from all over Tuscany competed in a jousting tournament for the honor of standing beside you in the Pazzi Chapel as your future husband. The winner will be arriving on this island any day now."

The voice from the hope chest said, "I want my wedding to take place in the cathedral."

"The cathedral? Well, I—"

"You said the Pazzi are going to make you an archbishop. An archbishop wearing a golden miter can arrange anything."

"That is true."

"And, after our wedding in the cathedral, I want us to repeat our vows in every church in Florence. No, every domed church in Florence."

"Yes, every domed church."

"On both sides of the Arno."

"Of course, that can be arranged."

Florentia sat up, like a bather in a tub, showing a head with all the hairiness of a coconut. "You say the winner of the jousting tournament will arrive in his armor any day now?"

"Any day now."

"But my hair! 'Any day now' is much too soon!"

. . .

Early next morning in the vegetable garden, Florentia tossed her rake aside to go whirling through the meadow in a white lace wedding gown designed by Sandro Botticelli, with additional touches by Michelangelo to give her a statuesque look. The meadow all around her sparkled with dew, every leaf and petal beaded from edge to edge. Bending low for a closer look at a leaf that was as packed with dewdrops as Florence was with domed churches, she began hearing church bells and seeing not dewdrops on a leaf but all the domed churches of Florence on the morning of her wedding. The large glistening dome in the center was the cathedral where her wedding would first take place. The domes around it were the churches where she and her husband would repeat their vows.

That vision sent her whirling again through the meadow, in even wider circles than before, the train of her bridal gown scattering dewdrops in all directions.

Enzo, on his way to the charnel house, waved to Florentia, but she did not see him. She was in Florence getting married, over and over.

. . .

Florentia was still whirling down the cobblestone streets of the meadow when Enzo stepped to the charnel house door flanked by cypresses standing sentry that did nothing to stop the man from pushing his way in. Renato was on his hands and knees with a bucket and brush, scrubbing the floor before inviting his friends to see what he had discovered beneath some broken tiles.

Seeing Enzo's grim expression, Renato thought, "He's come to tell me that my mother has died." The boy, starting to rise, dropped the brush in the pail. Enzo ordered him back on his knees. Believing the priest was about to kneel beside him in prayer, the boy said, "This is about my mother, isn't it?" Enzo shook his head. Renato, still seeing death in the man's eyes, said, "Please, don't tell me something's happened to Placido. Or Florentia."

"Yes, something has happened, something terrible," said Enzo. "Listen and you will learn. Soon after I arrived on this island, I took upon myself the care of two orphaned children. One of them was a girl not yet three years old. That girl has grown to be a young woman of marriageable age, and it is my duty as guardian to find her a suitable husband. I have found that young man."

The boy brightened. Enzo hadn't come with sad news. Just the opposite. Seeing love grow between Renato and Florentia, he had come to bless their union.

"The young man I have found is a Christian of fine family, who will guide Florentia along the path of salvation, far from the road to damnation down which you are leading her. A match worthy of her is being arranged right now in Florence. But because of your selfish desires, you are willing to destroy that young woman's one chance at happiness. Don't deny it. Don't shake your head. Don't say a word. You've imagined her being in this house of death with you. Haven't you?"

The words struck Renato like blows, and he collapsed to the floor and pressed his head against the soapy, wet tiles.

"It was her red hair, wasn't it, that made you fall so low," said Enzo, placing before the boy's reddened eyes something tied with string. "Don't turn away. Look at it. Do you know what she did because of you, knowing it was her red hair that tempted you to sin? She cut off all her beautiful hair." Renato, in agony, rubbed his face along the flooring stones, showing Enzo a tearful eye.

"You know what else she did, because of you? She took the blade of the scissors and turned it against herself. Yes, because of you. Your tears won't wash that away."

"You mean she—"

"No. I stopped her hand in time."

The boy, in gratitude, crept forward and kissed the man's shoe. Enzo pulled away, saying, "I promised Florentia I would go forward with plans for her wedding, if she kept herself pure. The fine husband chosen for her will be arriving here any day now. But you must do your part. Are you willing to sacrifice, for the sake of her happiness?"

"What do you want me to do?" asked the boy, his fingers sliding along the floor toward the lock of hair to save it from the beads of water all around it.

But Enzo covered it with his shoe and said, "What you must do is very simple. Stay away from her. Just stay away."

Ralph Feliciello

Part Three: The Temple of Venus

Chapter 8

Building a Boat

There, at Renato's feet, lay the child-size, earth-walled, windowless room sure to be occupied soon. There beside it, the mound of dirt that would become, at his hands, shovelful upon shovelful, the roof of that room. Renato stood there so long, shovel in hand, trying not to think of what was to come, that his shadow, begun at the shallow grave, now stretched to the far end of the cemetery. It was from there that the weeping came.

Dropping the shovel on the dirt mound, Renato moved toward the sound, his shadow leading the way until it darkened the Gibbet lying face down in the dirt, moaning, "Emiliano, my poor little Emiliano." Seeing Renato, he pressed his hand to his mouth as if to seal within words he had already spoken. "I did not say anything. You did not hear me say anything. I did not say a name. Go away from this place. We do not want you here." His withered hand reached for a rock half-buried in the earth, but the earth refused to let go. "Earth, you are too strong for me. Soon you will hold me, too, in your grasp."

Renato offered his hand. The Gibbet chose his cane instead and, jabbing at the earth, struggled to his feet. "Remember, boy, when you see your mother, you did not hear me say a name."

"His mother is standing here, by the open grave meant for her," said the Childwoman, appearing with the suddenness of a ghost. The Gibbet stabbed at the earth with his cane until he was at her side. "You should be in your bed."

"I'm tired of my bed. All I hear around my bed is death talk. Dying people want to hear beautiful lies that make them want to go on living. I heard what you said before. I heard everything you said. I heard you say the name. Now I have something to say I should have said long ago. Renato, leave your father and me. Go to the shack and wait there."

The Gibbet waited until Renato was too small to hear, then grumbled, "That boy left the shovel laying here in the dirt. He should have put it in the shed."

"Your precious shovel," she said, "your precious, precious shovel."

"Woman," he said, "you're speaking of the spoon that fed you." Reaching for the shovel, he lost his footing, his cane slipped out from under him, and he crumbled into the child-size grave. Half in, half out, he tried to raise himself but could not. "You should be laughing. People are supposed to laugh when somebody falls on his backside, especially in an empty grave." He held out his cane, hoping she would help him. The Childwoman closed her hand around the end of the cane but made no move to help. Staring from the blue veins of her hand to the blue veins of his, she uttered these terrible words, "You spoke his name."

"Help me," said the Gibbet.

"Renato heard you say the name. He's waiting for me in the shack. What am I supposed to tell him about that name?"

"Tell him nothing. We vowed never to speak of what happened."

"I will not tell Renato the truth, because as long as there is breath in this body he must know me, and only me, as his mother. I did not give birth to him but I gave him his name. Tell me why I gave Renato a name that means re-born."

Speaking from the grave, the Gibbet again said, "Help me."

The Childwoman yanked the cane away and flung it aside. "A long time ago, I asked you to help me when I could not leave my sickbed. I asked you to put your shovel aside so you could look after our baby. Maybe it was a blessing that he went to his grave before he could walk. But he could crawl, couldn't he?"

From the grave, "Help me."

She kicked dirt from the mound at her feet. "That's right. Swallow dirt, like you made our baby swallow dirt."

"I set him on his blue blanket at the base of a tree."

"So that you could go back to your shovel and finish filling in a grave. But, with the grave only half full—"

"The handle split, just above the blade."

"So, you went to the shed."

"I ran to the shed."

"For another shovel, then went back."

"I ran back. I could still run then."

"And you quickly finished filling in the grave that you had begun."

"So, I could play with my baby son."

"But when you turned to the tree, your baby son was not on the blanket."

"Smiling, I got down on all fours and crawled over the filled-in grave, calling out, 'Where are you, my little mischief? You're too young to be running away from home.'"

"But he didn't run away from home, did he? Did he?"

"Help me."

"Where could our baby son have gone? Tell me. Stop your sniveling and tell me where he was when you finally saw our baby son's face again."

The Gibbet used the shovel to pull himself out of the grave, then, letting the shovel fall, he embraced his weeping Childwoman who sobbed, "My breasts were laden! Laden!"

. . .

The nails that held Jesus on the cross had worked themselves loose. Renato was pressing the nail deeper into the left hand when he heard the Childwoman say, "I like the nails loose." Renato loosened the nail at the left hand and the right and the nail at the feet. "Please, put it back on the wall. The nail on the wall is loose, too. But no matter."

Renato set the crucifix on its nail. The Childwoman said, "You heard your father at the unmarked grave. You heard him say a name."

"Yes. I heard him say, 'My poor little—' "

She stopped him. "He should not have said the name. And I will tell you why. I will tell you everything. Walk with me a while. I'm feeling much better. It's nature's way of telling me I'll die soon." Renato, fingers pressed to his mother's forehead, said, "You're burning."

"That's me feeling hell's furnace firing up to receive me. Come. I want to see the ocean one more time."

They walked down the hill side by side, the difference in their height making them seem more father and child than mother and son. Hanging on his arm for support, she said, "You are a man now, Renato, a strong man. Who would have thought a sparrow would give birth to an eagle?"

Mother and son arrived at the place where the sea whitens the shore. She said, "Do you remember, when you were a little boy, no taller than I am, you saw my hair starting to turn white and said, 'What does it mean when a person's hair does that?' "

"Yes, I do remember and I remember your answer—that when a person's hair turns white it means the same thing it means for the sea when it turns white at the shore, that it's come to the end of its journey."

"My hair is whiter than ever now."

Renato said, "I don't want you to come to the end of your journey."

"Oh, but I've kept the devil waiting long enough. It won't do to make him angry. Look. The sun is just sitting on the horizon, waiting for me to tell you about the name that should never have been spoken, the name of your brother."

"My brother?"

"You were not alone inside of me. You came out of me first, and you were healthy and strong. The first thing you did was to hold up your little fist, like a conqueror. Your father saw you do that. And then he watched your little brother being pulled out of me, the most beautiful shade of blue you could ever hope to see, the birth cord wound around his neck. When your father saw the way that you came out and then the way your brother came out, the man lost his reason. He spent the next three days curled up on the floor of the shed behind the shovels. Since that day, the only person he ever trusted was the devil. And every time he looked at you, he saw your little fist in the air and he remembered what you did to little Emiliano inside of me."

"Mother, why didn't you ever tell me?"

"Who can speak of these things?"

Renato said, "If we told each other the truth, maybe we would all be a little happier."

"Nobody tells the truth, and nobody's happy. That's the truth. You happy now?"

"No."

"Look. The sun is gone. It was here a moment ago. Where could the sun have gone?"

Renato carried his mother up the hill and set her on her feet at the door of the cemetery shack. She said, "Thank you for our walk together. I wanted to see the ocean one more time. It looked the same."

. . .

Renato believed there must be a monastery on the island of Elba where monks with mortar and pestle mixed herbs and spiderwebs into potions able to make his mother well again. To bring her to Elba he would need a boat. But the last big storm had smashed a boat once moored to the dock, leaving nothing behind but a few lone pieces of driftwood floating in the surf. Renato would have to build a boat. To do that he needed wood. In the shed, there was only enough wood for a coffin.

Next morning, a little before sunrise, Renato was pondering the problem, walking back and forth along the water's edge, when the solution suddenly came to him like a ball of fire rising into the sky. Later, shirtless in the sun, he attacked the shed with the claw of his hammer, removing board after board. Splinters buried themselves under his skin. He could see them but he had to keep on working.

"Pulcinella, you'll have to straighten every nail then hammer every board back in place," said the Gibbet. Stepping over the fallen boards, he said, "Come and say goodbye to your mother. But she won't be able to hear you."

Renato still had the hammer in his hand when he brushed past the black cassock to reach the bed where his mother lay very still, her head resting on the pillow between lighted candles, making her face seem whiter than usual. Her hands, joined on her chest, held the crucifix whose nails were so loose the figure on the cross might have slipped off, if not held so tightly.

"I performed the Last Rites. She is with God now," said a voice.

Renato dropped to his knees beside the bed and, looking into his mother's closed eyes, said, "You don't understand. I'm building a boat. On Elba there are monks with mortars and pestles who can—"

He could go no further. He felt a consoling hand on his shoulder. Someone was helping him to his feet. He pressed his sobbing face to hers, trying to say the words, "But I'm building a boat."

Chapter 9

Silence and the Grave

They gathered around the Childwoman's grave under so light a rain that individual drops did not fall but lingered in the air above the mourners, like dust particles drifting through space without order or purpose.

The Gibbet was the first to depart. Enzo read words from a black book, closed the book, pressed it with both hands against the too-many buttons of his cassock, then he, too, departed.

Placido tried to think of something to say to Renato that would ease his friend's pain, but, notwithstanding that he knew many more words than Renato, he found only these to say—"The rain seems to have slowed down." Florentia embraced Renato, and Placido embraced them both, as if to press on them that the three friends would always be together. After a parting touch to his friend's shoulder and his sister's hand, Placido walked on alone down the hill, his eyes on the horizon and his mind on the sea, the accumulated tears of all mankind.

Florentia and Renato alone remained, silence and the grave between them. Fingering the ends of her black scarf, she watched his fingers tighten around the crucifix he held upside down in his hand. The posy of wildflowers in her hand was hanging upside down when she said, "She didn't like me."

"That's not true," said Renato.

"She thought I was trying to seduce you."

"Oh, yes, for all my millions," he said and got down on one knee to set the crucifix upright on the grave then began placing white stones around the foot of the cross, saying, "I am so sorry for your pain."

"Life was not kind to her," said Florentia.

"I mean your pain," he said.

"You're sorry for my pain?"

"Yes, you cut off your hair because of me then turned the blade of the scissors against yourself."

The wildflowers fell from Florentia's hand. She sank to her knees before Renato and, looking into his sadness, said, "You never hurt me, ever. And I never tried to hurt myself. That's another one of Enzo's lies. I cut off my hair because you made me happy, and I didn't want to be happy." Saying the word "happy" made her cry. Renato drew her to him and wiped away her tears. She did the same for him, then together they arranged the wildflowers one by one around the white stones holding the crucifix in place.

Ralph Feliciello

. . .

Placido was wandering along the shore when the monthly supply boat appeared. As the vessel drew nearer, he saw it was not the usual boat but a skiff which, with dark clouds gathering, seemed hardly up to the journey. The familiar face of the man tossing him the mooring rope set the boy at ease. "You're two weeks early," said Placido.

"This day is many years too late," Half Mast replied. "The citizens of Florence have emptied Palazzo Medici of traitors and looted their treasures. Your family is back from exile in Paris, Master Pazzi, and I've come to deliver you to them. It's all happened as you heard Signor Farfalla say it would. Step aboard."

"What about Father Enzo?" asked Placido. "I can't leave without him."

"Don't worry yourself, Master. A second boat is coming for him. It will be here soon. My orders are to bring you back immediately. A great banquet is being prepared in your honor at Palazzo Pazzi. Every campanile in Florence will burst its bells welcoming you home. But we must hurry," he said, planting his foot on the gunwale and offering Placido a helping hand.

"I want to say goodbye to my sister."

"She's not your sister, remember?" said Half Mast, taking hold of the boy's wrist.

Placido said, "But there's a storm on the way." That was when Half Mast placed something in his new master's hand that widened the boy's eyes. Placido stepped willingly over the gunwale and sat down at the bow.

Half Mast was saying, "When we stormed Palazzo Medici, I grabbed what you have in your hand from Lorenzo de' Medici's personal art collection. You're a rich man now, Master Pazzi. You can collect many more Roman art treasures, just like that. It's made of, ah—"

"Sardonyx," said Placido, not lifting his eyes from the ancient cameo.

"Yes. What you said. Many might not know its value."

"It's priceless," whispered Placido breathless with admiration for the gemstone delicately carved in three receding layers, tan, white, and brown, showing Venus holding the Golden Apple of the Hesperides, her prize for being judged more beautiful than Juno and Minerva.

By the time Placido raised his eyes again from the jewel beyond price that Lorenzo de' Medici himself must have held in the palm of his hand, Pianosa Island had sunk below the horizon.

Placido, from his place in the bow, regarded the man who had called him "Master," reasoning that the sullen look on Half Mast's face was a consequence of the great difference in their stations in life. The lowborn resent their betters. One must get used to that unfortunate fact.

"Keep your head down, Master Pazzi," warned Half Mast, "or you're liable to suffer a nasty hit on the head. I mean, with the wind acting up, the boom might suddenly swing around."

Placido, examining the cameo more carefully, noticed something that convinced him there was no banquet waiting for him at Palazzo Pazzi, more likely the Black Death was waiting at Half Mast's docking place, sword in hand. Seconds later, Half Mast was shouting, "Come back, Master," seeing his reward money swimming away. "Come back! You'll never make it to shore!" But Placido—who, Renato joked, swam like a stone—kept churning his arms and legs in the direction where the island once rose above the horizon, praying it would soon appear.

By the time the belfry of the campanile did raise its head, Placido's legs felt like two marble columns.

The Birth of Venus

Carrying a sputtering candle that did more to blind the holder than light the way before him, Renato led Florentia down the darkened stairs he had discovered under the charnel house floor. Florentia, with blackness all around her, said, "I feel like a piece of coal sinking in a vat of tar."

"It gets worse," he said.

"Wonderful."

The final step of the stairway set the leader and then his follower on a walkway curving deep into the darkness. Florentia, certain that the next step would send her tumbling off the edge of the earth, dug her nails into Renato's arm. "Please, take me back. I want to go back. I'm scared."

"Only a few more steps."

"The walls are closing in on us."

"The spirals of the walkway are making tighter turns because we're getting close. We're almost at the entrance. All right, I'll take you back."

"Wait. How close is 'almost'?"

"One more turn."

"One more turn?"

"One more turn."

"All right. One more turn."

One more turn, and a bronze door appeared, green with age.

"We're here. I'll open the door. As you walk in, you should have your eyes closed. Are they closed?"

"No," she said. "I'll close them, but don't let go of my hand!"

"I need both hands to open the door."

Renato's footfalls moved away. Then came the scream of a heavy door scraping across the stone floor. Renato was holding her hand again. "Come. Not such baby steps. Good. You're inside now. I'm walking you to the center of the room. It's a circular room, so it's easy to find the center. You're standing in the center of the room now. Open your eyes."

"I don't want to be disappointed. Will I be disappointed?"

"You might be. You're in a completely empty room. There's nothing but a round floor, circular walls, and a domed ceiling."

Florentia willed her eyes to open, slowly. And she saw she was in an enchanted wood of fruit-bearing trees—apple, pear, orange, cherry, apricot, pomegranate, and more, and all as heavy with delights as the first day the sun rose above Eden. "Oh, I'd love to take a bite of that peach!" she cried.

"Careful, you're headed for a stream."

"I don't care," she said, kicking across a brook where red-and-white fish darted this way and that, not caring where they were going.

"Aren't you lovely," she told a spotted fawn keeping close to her mother. Florentia bent down to pet a floppy-eared rabbit, while nearby a mother goose led a row of waddling goslings.

"I agree you are very handsome," Florentia told a peacock displaying his maleness in all its glory.

The room, as Renato had said, was empty, empty of objects, yet Rome's finest masters of mosaic art had transformed the circular floor into a living meadow that rose to a panoramic fresco where birds on the wing lighted on fruit-laden trees all pointing to a painted dome where sun, moon, and stars beamed down on a world of peace and plenty.

"The candle will go out soon," said Renato, "but you must see one more thing." And he led Florentia to an arched alcove—an apse, as Placido would have correctly named it. There she beheld a fresco of the deity whose temple this was—Venus, goddess of Love and Abundance, floating on a half shell, led by a boy on a dolphin. As Placido would have explained, Venus was naked simply because she had just been born fully formed from the foam of the sea.

"Is it just the candle flame flickering, or did Venus just turn to me, about to speak?"

"Maybe she wants you to speak first. People usually ask gods—"

"Or goddesses," put in Florentia.

"—or goddesses, to help them. Ask her if she will help us get to the New World."

A moment passed and Florentia said, "I asked her."

"And what did she say?"

"She wanted to know first if we believed in her, if we worshipped her, if we were lovers. When I answered Yes, she promised she would send us to the New World, by setting each of us on a leaping dolphin that will carry us over the sea—if our love proves true."

Renato set the candle down in the meadow beside the rabbit. "Since we are here in the temple of Venus," he began, "and we are lovers, as you said...."

"But the candle will go out soon," said Florentia, "I think we'd better—"

"We're in the temple of Love," said Renato. "No thinking allowed."

"Well, then," said Florentia, bringing her face close to the candle whose flame doubled itself in her eyes.

His voice said, "You blew out the candle."

Her voice said, "Yes, I did."

His voice, "How will we find our way back?"

Her voice, "By feel."

His: "When we stopped what we were doing in the hollow tree, what was it that we were doing, exactly?"

Hers: "I think it was this."

His: "This is good. I like this. But I believe it was this."

Then both voices together said, "Yes, this was definitely it."

One thing led, as it so often does, to another, and soon, under the eyes of Venus, who could see very clearly in the dark, Renato and Florentia began worshipping the goddess in the same way lovers always have and always will.

. . .

Their worship completed, Florentia and Renato left the underground temple to stroll barefoot at the water's edge in the lingering blush of sunset. They needed no mosaic meadow to know they lived in an enchanted world, with the sun dipping low to be nearer to them and the sea bubbling in to caress their toes, again and again as they walked.

They spoke only with the touch of one hand upon another, telling of their future together in the New World. The more outlandish the plan, the more certain they were of its fulfillment. For the present, Florentia will quit the rectory to live with Renato in the charnel house which he promised to make more livable by fashioning a table and chairs out of wood stripped from the shed.

Florentia, separating her fingers from his, said, "There is something I must tell you."

"Can we kiss while you tell me?"

"You can kiss me after I tell you, if you still want to."

He said, "I'm sure that I will still—"

"Renato, you were not born on this island."

"I know. I hatched out of a sparrow's egg."

"Listen to me, just listen," she said, pressing a finger to his lips. "When you were a baby, Enzo carried you here from Florence. You are the one they call the Pazzi boy."

Renato bent down, selected several stones for flatness and weight, and sent one of them skimming over the water. "I know who I am," he said. "I am the gravedigger of Pianosa Island."

"You are the only heir of Jacopo de' Pazzi."

"I am my mother's son," he said, sending another stone skipping toward the horizon.

"Renato, the Pazzi family, your family, will be coming for you soon. But Enzo's plan is to have Placido take your place."

"It's not my place, if I don't want it," said Renato. "Placido can have my place."

"The richest and most beautiful city in Italy is preparing to welcome you."

"I don't want to live in that world. I want to live in a New World, with you."

"You could have your choice of any woman in Florence."

"I want a woman named Florentia. But Enzo has a plan for her, too, and it doesn't include me."

"Renato, I am never, ever, going back to the rectory or to any plan Enzo has for me. I want to be with you."

"With me in palazzo charnel house?"

"Yes, in palazzo charnel house."

"Then, I can kiss you now," he said and he did. The kiss was not quite completed when the kiss-ee, having more to say, began kiss-saying, "Promise me that nothing could ever make you hate me."

"I hate you now, for what you did to your hair. You look like—"

Florentia ran off laughing toward a clump of seaweed tumbling in the surf, crying out over her shoulder as she ran, "We needn't wait for my hair to grow back. I can have a full head of green hair right now. Would you like me with green hair?"

"Maybe better," yelled Renato, hurrying after her. "Green hair will match your eyes. Well, one of them."

Up ahead, Florentia slowed to a stop, as if ordered to halt. For it was not seaweed alone that had washed up on shore.

. . .

Enzo rose from his favorite chair, seeing Renato blur past the open door carrying Placido in his arms, then Florentia rushed by breathlessly saying something that might have been, "He's breathing."

In Placido's room, Renato lowered his friend onto the bed.

"The Last Rites," said Enzo. "I'll get the—"

"No need," said Renato. "Remember last summer when I pulled him half-drowned out of the undertow? An hour later he was sitting up in bed asking for a book to read." Florentia, smiling at the memory, touched Renato's arm. He pulled away from her and left the rectory at such an angry pace that pebbles shot up from his heels, to discourage Florentia from following behind. She pursued him, without saying a word, all the way up the hill to the cemetery, where he grabbed a shovel leaning against a tree and began digging and shoveling dirt aside. Florentia stood her ground as black rainbows arced between them.

"Please say something." No answer. "I know you're angry with me," she said, moving closer.

In the twilight between love and hate, Renato stabbed at rocks embedded in the ground, sending deadly sparks flying up at Florentia, only to become fireflies and disappear around her.

"Please, tell me why you are angry with me."

Renato grabbed the shaft of the shovel and, hoisting it aloft like a spear aimed at the heart of an enemy, said, "You're going back to the rectory, aren't you."

"Yes, I'm going back. I know I swore I would never go back, but—"

"That must be the shortest never since time began."

"My brother needs me."

"No. It's not what Placido needs. It's what Florentia needs, and Florentia needs Enzo, because Enzo is going to make her a fine lady of Florence. That's what you really want, isn't it? So, go. Go to your fine, new husband."

"You fool. I already have a husband. Enzo is my husband, or might as well have been. You would have seen it, if you weren't living in a dream world. Dreamer, open your eyes."

Renato threw the shovel to the ground. "My eyes are open now, and I don't like what I see."

"Look, the stars are starting to fill the sky, like the night you were spying on me from the bluff. Do you know why I waded out into the water to pray to the moon?"

"That doesn't matter to me now."

"No, because to you the moon is something distant, up there, far away. But the moon moves here inside of my body, moves my blood. All during the last moon my blood did not flow. I was scared. Do you understand?"

"No," he said and started to walk away.

Florentia, trembling, grabbed his arm and told him, face to face, "You must hear this. The moon heard my prayers that night, and blood began flowing inside of me again, the day you kissed me in my room."

"Yes, well, that was a mistake," said Renato, picking up the shovel. "Now, I have work to do. And you need to go back to the rectory to keep paying Enzo his fee for being such an excellent matchmaker, and at such a low price." He raised the shovel and, pressing the blade against his enemy, pushed her to the ground. "Good. That's where you belong, in the dirt. I was so ashamed of the dirt under my nails. But you are dirt." He picked up a handful of dirt to throw at her but let it fall through his fingers and offered his hand.

Motioning him away, Florentia saw the Gibbet jabbing at the earth on his way to the unmarked grave. He told her, "Girl, don't get in the way of my son's work. He has to dig my grave." He continued on, with Florentia shouting after him, "Be Renato's father for the first time in your life and tell that boy the truth. He has a right to know!"

"Did you tell him the truth?"

"Yes, I did."

"And did he thank you for it?"

She got to her feet, brushed the dirt from her clothes, and ran from the graveyard.

When Florentia arrived at the rectory, Enzo was waiting for her in the doorway. As she brushed by him, he said, "I knew you'd be back."

Chapter 10

The Black Death Returns

R enato was wrong. An hour went by, and Placido did not sit up and ask for a book to read. It seemed certain it was Enzo who would be reading, from his black book, the prayers for the dead. The vigil at Placido's bedside continued for two days and nights that Florentia spent sitting in a bedside chair, sleep at times overtaking her.

On the morning of the third day, Placido opened his eyes. Seeing his sister slumped in the chair, with the wall for a pillow, he realized that he was in his own room and not at the bottom of the sea in the stomach of a whale or a giant octopus, sloshing around with the remains of half-digested crustaceans.

He saw his clothes draped over the desk chair and thought of checking if the cameo was still in his pocket but, on hearing Enzo calling out for Florentia to sew a button on his cassock, Placido lowered his eyelids. He sensed Florentia rising from the chair, felt her fingers on his forehead, and heard her say, "Placido, you've worried us for much too long. Jump out of that bed right now and stop this lazing about, leaving all the chores to me." Her fingers left his forehead, and he heard her shouting to Enzo that she would get her sewing basket and bring it to the study.

Enzo was straightening the Madonna and Child when Florentia, not happy to have been taken from her brother's bedside, sat down on the bench and plopped the sewing basket on her lap. Enzo set three black buttons spinning on the bench beside her. She waited for the last button to wobble then come to rest on the bench, and said, "You told me 'a button.' I see three there."

"Yes," said Enzo, planting his foot beside the buttons, "but since this is the last duty I will ever ask of my housekeeper...."

Florentia, after rummaging through the sewing basket, began poking the needle in the eye. Enzo, gazing up to heaven through the ceiling of the study and the roof of the rectory, recited, "It is easier for a rich man to enter the Kingdom of—"

His housekeeper corrected him. "It is easier for a camel to pass through...."

"Right you are," said Enzo. "You have been well catechized. It is easier for a camel to pass through the eye of a needle than for a rich man to enter the Kingdom of Heaven."

"Meaning," offered Florentia, "that it is not easy for a rich man to enter the Kingdom of Heaven, but he can easily shorten his stay in Purgatory to, say, a week or two, if he could pay the price."

"You should be concentrating on your work and not my sinful past. Well, all that is behind me now: 'Get thee behind me, Satan.' Who was it who said that?"

In Florentia's hands, the thread passed through the eye of the needle as easily as Saint Francis strolled through the Gates of Heaven. With the threaded needle in one hand and the hem of the cassock in the other, she said, "Stay still," and speared a button through its black heart.

"Careful!" cried Enzo who cleared his throat and took a moment to compose himself before stating, "The time has finally come for us to go our separate ways. I will leave this island with a clear conscience. I served out the penance the Pope assigned me. I kept my promise to Signora Pazzi and carried the child out of harm's way. And everyone on this island will benefit from what I have done here. Your brother will open his eyes to a rich and cultured future he would never have known without me. And, if there is any justice in this world, I will, before long, be balancing an archbishop's miter on my head. Excuse me, are you intentionally stabbing me in the shin with that needle?"

"No."

"And, for you, a wedding in the cathedral of Florence and a life, pampered by servants, as the signora of a palazzo shaded in summer by the cathedral's magnificent dome. Everyone benefits."

"Aren't you forgetting a certain young man, born in a palazzo, who sleeps in the charnel house, because of you?"

Enzo yanked his foot from the bench. "That boy is alive today because of me. On the day of his birth, I carried him out of Florence, at no small risk to myself."

"Put your foot back on the bench," she said.

Enzo did as he was told, saying, "His own family handed him to me like a bundle of laundry and ran off to Paris. I brought him here expecting your mother to be his nurse. When she died, he went to the Childwoman who, as luck would have it, had been nursing an infant of her own. If Renato is sleeping in the charnel house now, it was not of my choosing. I did what the Pazzi family asked me to do, and Fate did the rest. In any case, he is content with his lot. Everyone is happy."

"Oh, yes, everyone is perfectly happy!" cried Florentia. Her eyes blurred with tears, she knocked the sewing basket to the floor, snatched up the scissors, and sent them flying end over end across the room, her scream powerless to stop the blade from landing like a dagger between Mother and Child. Stumbling to the doorway she fell sobbing into Renato's arms.

He withdrew from her, and all turned toward the welcome sound of a wide-awake voice coming from Placido's room. Renato said, "That is the voice I came to hear. I can go now," and he left the rectory, never to return.

. . .

Placido, sitting up in bed, content after what he described as the best meal of his life, handed the cameo to Florentia and explained why he had decided it was safer to chance a watery death than remain in the skiff with Half Mast.

"I realized he was lying. That cameo could not have come from Lorenzo de' Medici's personal collection. The workmanship is second-rate. It shows The Judgment of Paris in three receding layers, yes, but incorrectly. Venus, judged by the Prince of Troy to be the most beautiful goddess of all, should have been carved into the chestnut-colored foremost layer, not the white middle layer more appropriate for the two losers of the beauty contest, Juno and Minerva. As soon as I saw that, I dove in and swam below the surface as far from the skiff as I could until I had to come up for air and spit out a mouthful of seawater."

Placido thanked his sister again for the meal that had tasted, "extraordinarily good, except it was, perhaps, a little too salty."

Adam and Eve Forgiven

Renato knew that, though his friend survived Half Mast's failed kidnap attempt, The Black Death was sure to return for one last attempt to trade Placido's life for a coffin full of florins.

That afternoon Renato climbed the tallest oak on the island, bough after bough after bough, until he was lying face down on the highest branch strong enough to support his weight. He kept his eyes focused, beyond the leaves at the end of the bough, on his old enemy the horizon. The first day at his lookout post, nothing disturbed the long, black line separating sea from sky. The second day, the same.

On the third, all he saw moving among the leaves at the end of the branch was a white butterfly fluttering its wings. Looking closer he saw not the wings of a butterfly but the billowing sails of a ship, distant but fast approaching. He must hurry and sound the alarm. Turning suddenly, he heard a crack, felt the bough give way beneath him, and fell from branch to branch to branch until he could at last hold fast, then drop the final ten feet to the ground, his ankle buckling under him in the dirt.

By the time a panting Renato paused to catch his breath at the bottom of the hill, the ship was alongside the pier. With no time to knock at the rectory door, he ran to the campanile, spiraled up the staircase to the belfry, grabbed the knotted bell rope, and put it to good use. The rectory door flew open, and three upturned faces appeared at the foot of the campanile.

No need for words. All eyes could see soldiers forming into ranks on the pier and The Black Death on his black steed galloping toward the Pazzi boy. Renato jumped from the belfry onto the sloping church roof, slid upright to the brink, launched himself into the air, and unhorsed the unsuspecting condottiere who ended on his backside with his own longsword pointed at his heart.

Suddenly, Renato was wearing a necklace of spear points. The Black Death, rising to his feet, called off his men, saying with a smile, "Didn't I tell you this boy would make a good soldier one day?"

Signor Farfalla fluttered in to assure Renato he need not fear the condottiere. "This soldier-for-hire now serves Florence's new masters," he said, pointing to the ship's mast flying the Pazzi flag with its pair of leaping dolphins, tails flapping in the breeze.

Farfalla waited for the Pazzi family to gather around him, and then proclaimed, "The citizens of Florence have taken back their Republic! Never again will Medici tyrants trample on our liberty!"

Cheers lasting longer than Farfalla was willing to go without hearing his own voice, he called for silence, turned his caterpillar eyebrows to Placido, and said, "Young man, I have the privilege of representing the noble Pazzi clan, here to welcome you, scion of the family." A woman with kind eyes introduced herself to Placido as the sister of Signora Pazzi who, sadly, passed away a week before the family left Paris. "I am your Aunt Monica," she said. "May I be the first in the family to embrace you?" She opened her arms to Placido who, after encouraging nods from Renato and Florentia, accepted her embrace, to shouts of approval joined by the joyful banging of many hands together, some in the crowd pausing to wipe away a tear.

"And now," said Signor Farfalla, "let me bring forward a very special individual who has something important to say to someone who— well, I will let him tell you himself." The group parted to make way for the Archbishop of Florence, clad in full archbishopric splendor, wearing a golden miter that reached for Heaven but made it only halfway. His Excellency, holding in his white-gloved, many-ringed hand a crystalline shepherd's crook, called out, "Come stand before me, Father Scallappetti," and he hooked the crook around Enzo's neck and separated him from the crowd. "Rejoice with me, people," he said, "for I have found my sheep which was lost." And the people rejoiced with him.

"I am pleased to report, Father Scallapetti, believing that you have suffered long enough here in your Purgatory on earth, that your next assignment will be in a faraway land, not yet named on any map, where savages have already graced several missionaries with martyrdom." Some in the crowd lifted their hands to applaud but, somewhat bewildered, finished by joining their palms together in prayer.

His Excellency went on to say, mischief dancing in his eyes, "But I jest. Father, for your next assignment you shall be...allowed to return to your old post in the Pazzi Chapel. You seem surprised, Father." Enzo, who was all the while praying the archbishop would lift the miter from his own head and place it on Enzo's to crown the good work he had done, sputtered, "Yes, I am surprised—at your magnanimity."

Signor Farfalla took back control of the proceedings to make a special announcement. "At this time, the Pazzi family wishes to show its heartfelt gratitude to you, young lady." And he looked to Florentia who looked to Renato who looked away.

"Because you cared for Placido as if he were your own flesh and blood, the family has arranged for you a match with one of our most distinguished noblemen, as whose wife you will become the signora of the finest palazzo in Florence, recently and hastily vacated by its former owners. I speak of none other than...Palazzo Medici. And now—"

After the applause quieted, Farfalla repeated his last two words so the world would not be deprived of them. "And now...before we embark on our return voyage, let us proceed to the church and bow our heads, as His Excellency leads us in a prayer of thanksgiving."

Only then, as Florentia joined the procession, with Placido nudging her elbow, did she realize that Renato was nowhere to be seen.

. . .

Renato left the charnel house carrying a sack of bones that held so little meaning for him now that he let it drag over the graves to the back of the cemetery. He was about to toss the sack down the sinkhole when the Gibbet, coming up behind, moved the boy aside with his knobby cane and hobbled on. Renato watched the man jabbing at the earth, each jab bringing to mind another word Florentia had flung at the Gibbet to "tell-that-boy-the-truth-he-has-a-right-to-know."

Renato caught up with his father, took hold of his wrist, and walked beside him, the cane leaving pockmarks in the dirt between them.

"Where are you taking me? You're hurting me."

"I want you to help me find a good place to bury this sack of bones," said Renato pressing on past a grave marked by a crucifix, past the skeletons of trees, the last skeleton holding on its outstretched fingers a bird's nest.

Stopping at the end of the cemetery, Renato dropped the sack of bones on the unmarked grave and said, "How about here, father? This looks like a good place to dig."

"Not here, not here," begged the Gibbet with a hand on his heart.

"Why not here? There's no one buried here, is there? I see no cross, no flowers."

"You know very well someone's buried here," said the Gibbet, dropping to his knees.

"But I don't know his name. Tell me his name. Say the name. I need to hear you say the name. I'll help you: 'My poor little—'"

"—little Emiliano," moaned the Gibbet, and his hand went again to his heart.

"You never told me what happened to poor little Emiliano. But I know already. Mother told me."

"Your mother did not tell you. She vowed never to speak of it."

"She did speak of it. But I need to hear the truth from you."

"My heart, my heart."

"What happened to little Emiliano? Tell me, father."

"It was an accident! A terrible accident!" cried the Gibbet, stretching his arms out in the dirt and embracing his baby son.

"Yes, it was an accident," said Renato. "That is the truth. I needed to hear you say that. Thank you, father. Thank you."

"My heart, my heart," groaned the Gibbet, crawling away from the grave.

Renato lifted his father up and carried him like a baby, kissing the baby's face flecked with dirt and telling him along the way to the shack, "It's all right. It's all right."

By the time he lowered his father's head to the pillow, Renato had become an orphan for the second time, though to him it was the first and only time, and he said to the head on the pillow, "They tried to tell me you were not my father, that some rich man in a palazzo was my father. But I know who my father is and I know who my mother is. And I know I had a little brother named Emiliano. What happened to my little brother in my mother's womb was an accident. You said so yourself a moment ago in the cemetery. Why you blamed me all those years, I don't understand. Because I was very young at the time, not even born yet, and didn't really know what I was doing. You could have just forgiven me, the way God maybe could have just forgiven Adam and Eve who were also very young at the time."

Two Leaping Dolphins

Renato carried his father to the windowless room he had prepared for him halfway between the unmarked grave and one where a crucifix leaned so far over that the figure hanging loose on the cross was in danger of falling to the earth.

He patted down the roof of the room with the flat of his shovel, laid the implement of his and his father's profession lengthwise on the grave, and placed the knobby cane across it, to mark the grave.

Before leaving the island, Renato took a moment to say goodbye to the only family he had ever known, his words falling so softly that they reached the ground but no further.

"I am sorry to leave you. When I was little, I thought we would always be together. But I am going now to a new land across the sea, where people live simply. That is how I want to live. But I promise I will be back someday to see you. I'm sure, when I do come back, we will have a lot to talk about."

Renato had never walked so slowly down the hill, past the hollow tree, and through the meadow where poppies reached up to touch his hand, waved to him after he had passed, and continued waving as the boy, small in the distance, stood at the edge of the bluff. They did not stop waving until he disappeared down the slope leading to the sea.

At the shore, Renato turned to let his eyes wander for the last time over the vegetable garden. Then he turned to the horizon and walked into the water.

. . .

The three-masted vessel flying the Pazzi flag got underway as family members young and old thronged around Placido. Men clapped him on the back. Women took turns embracing him, while Paris-born Pazzi children, yelping in their native French, welcomed him like excited puppies.

A young girl at the railing shouted, "Look! Two dolphins! Leaping clear out of the water!"

Placido, turning to his Aunt Monica, said, "Just the way they do on your flag," and she replied, "It's your flag, too."

Suddenly, someone at the opposite railing yelled, "Man overboard!" And all rushed to see a young man not fallen overboard but swimming with determined strokes toward the horizon. Placido called out, "Where are you going, my friend? Come aboard, for one minute. Renato, please!" The children cried, "*S'il vous plaît! S'il vous plaît! S'il vous plaît!*"

A rope ladder thrown over the side brought Renato on deck where he shook out his dripping hair like a shaggy dog after a dip, much to the children's delight. Placido briefly raised his hand in the air, and all the talkers became listeners. "My dear family," he began, "may I introduce to you my good friend—Amerigo."

"But," Aunt Monica leaned in to say, "you called him Renato a moment ago."

"On the island, we loved inventing nicknames for people. We used to call Father Scallappetti the Raven."

"I didn't know that," said Enzo, pressing so close to the archbishop he seemed to be trying to insert his head into the golden miter already fully occupied. The archbishop, looking to Placido, said, "But where is the young lady, the bride-to-be, the future signora of Palazzo Medici?"

Placido, pointing back to the island, said, "She's there, standing at the end of the pier. We thought she was coming with us, but she said something about Venus having a different plan for her." Before Placido had uttered the word Venus, Amerigo was back in the water, and Florentia was diving off the pier toward him.

Aunt Monica assured Placido there was room for two more passengers to Florence, but he was quite sure the couple had another destination in mind. Monica, holding her nephew's hand in hers, said, "My dear boy, how can we repay you for all you have suffered because of us? What would make you happy? Nothing will be denied you." Placido, looking to the horizon, said, "I would like to make a great voyage on a ship like this one."

"And where would you go on your great voyage?"

Someone at the bow called out, "Look! Two more dolphins!"

Placido pointed to a vision, that the goddess Venus allowed only to him, of a young man and a young woman, each riding a dolphin arcing clear over the horizon. "I'd like," said Placido, "to go where they are going."

"And where is that?" she asked.

"To the New World."

A boy began gently strumming a stringed instrument Placido had only heard in a woodcut in the pages of a book. The children joined hands and voices in sweet harmony, and Placido turned and watched as, far beyond the ship's widening wake, the island of his childhood drifted further and further away, diminishing in all dimensions, until there was very little to see and then nothing but endless sky floating upon an endless sea.

Fiction and Fact

Fiction: Jacopo de' Pazzi sired an illegitimate son that Lorenzo de' Medici ordered killed.

Fact: Ser Jacopo sired an illegitimate daughter, Caterina, who became a nun and was beatified. Another Caterina de' Pazzi, a century later, was canonized as Saint Maria Maddalena.

Fiction: A Roman underground temple to the goddess Venus was discovered under the charnel house on Pianosa Island.

Fact: The Roman fresco that inspired the episode in the temple, and the book's cover, can be viewed at the House of Venus in Pompeii.

Fiction: The priest who secreted the Pazzi baby out of Florence had been defrocked for selling papal indulgences promising the buyer a reduced sentence in purgatory.

Fact: The practice of selling indulgences under Pope Leo X, son of Lorenzo de' Medici, was motivated by the need to finance the construction of a new Saint Peter's Basilica. Martin Luther exposed abuses of the practice in his *Ninety-five Theses*.

Fiction: A condottiere known as The Black Death was charged with carrying out Lorenzo's death order against the Pazzi boy.

Fact: Condottieri, military commanders for hire, operated from medieval times to the mid-16th century. See the equestrian statue of Gattamelata by Donatello (Padua, 1453) and that of Bartolomeo Colleoni by Verrocchio (Venice, 1488).

Florentia and the Pazzi Boy

Further Reading

Harold Acton
The Pazzi Conspiracy: The Plot against the Medici
Thames and Hudson

Giovanni Boccaccio
The Decameron
Penguin Classics

Joseph Jay Deiss
Captains of Fortune: Profiles of Six Italian Condottieri
Cromwell / Gollancz

Pierre Louis Duchartre
The Italian Comedy / Commedia dell'Arte
Dover Publications

Deny Hay (Editor)
The Age of the Renaissance
McGraw-Hill

Christopher Hibbert
The House of Medici: Its Rise and Fall
Harper Perennial

Margaret L. King
Women of the Renaissance
The University of Chicago Press

Umberto Pappalardo
Greek and Roman Mosaics: Centurion Edition
Abbeville Press

Umberto Pappalardo
The Splendor of Roman Wall Painting
J. Paul Getty Museum

Ralph Feliciello, born in Mount Vernon, New York, grew up within an Italian-American family that had immigrated, early in the twentieth century, from small towns northeast of Naples. He spent his early years in the El Sereno neighborhood of northeast Los Angeles, later lived in San Francisco and Rome, and now makes his home in Queens, New York.

FlorentiaPazziBoy@gmail.com

Facebook.com/FlorentiaPazziBoy

Instagram/felicielloralph

Also by the author, writing as
R. L. Feliciello

3 American Cranks
a comic romp in three wildly eccentric voices
sounding off on life and love in today's America
gone haywire.

*"Timely and absolutely unique, studded with striking,
insightful, and hilarious gems—the result of mixing the DNA of
Fred Sanford, Arthur Rimbaud, and Henry Miller. Worthy of a
high place on the literary totem pole."*

Jason Rosette, author of
William Bonney's Electric Book of Hours and Bookwars

www.ingramcontent.com/pod-product-compliance
Lightning Source LLC
Chambersburg PA
CBHW020616130626
46552CB00014B/629